Forbidden Journey
When Worlds Collide

Patrick DiCicco

Copyright © 2017 Patrick DiCicco

All rights reserved. No part of this book may be reproduced or transmitted in any form or by any means, electronic or mechanical, including photocopying, recording or by any information storage and retrieval system, without permission in writing from the publisher.
P & D Publishing – Bakersfield, CA
ISBN 978-0-692-92343-6
Library of Congress Card Catalogue Number: 2017950904
DiCicco, Patrick
Forbidden Journey/ Patrick DiCicco
Available Formats: eBook | Paperback distribution

The Cover models/artwork...FJ Portraits of Campbell, Ohio

DEDICATION

This book is dedicated to the many dreamers who believe we are not alone, that there is another presence in the universe, and who believe life and love are eternal. The cast of characters in this book are very lifelike, whether alien or human, and are dedicated from a list of friends whom I know and have known. There is an Isaac and Diana in everyone of us; it just has to be discovered. And yet, though we may search, you must find your own place in the universe.

Introduction

The steel doors clanged loudly behind me, shutting off the world as I knew it. I was led in by an android with my arms limp by my side, as psychotropic drugs, local anesthesia and nerve induction replaced handcuffs long ago. I was now standing in a large circular atrium, which was the center of six long corridors, as if I was in the center of a hub. The ceiling was silicon treated plexiglass, exposing the starlit universe. This was the only mind altering and brain chip correctional facility in this sector, which housed both criminals and the few that couldn't handle the monotonous years in space. Some called it a floating hospital, some called it a prison. And some called it a living nightmare; nevertheless, it served as an institution for a multitude of starships in this galactic region. But it wasn't as I imagined either. There was no mulling around of inmates, or uncontrollable screaming, just an emptiness that gripped my soul.

Chapter One
Incarceration

It gave me some comfort to see the android escorting me was made in our image because other species from other planets occupied this facility too. He was seven feet tall, thinly built, with an elongated skull. As we walked the corridor, the drone of the nuclear engines eliminated any other sound and made it difficult to hear the android when he spoke. Then came a deafening silence as we entered the room. It was a large room with a glass office in the middle of it. It was occupied by thirty or more figures sitting on the perimeter walls, all sitting in their chair like vegetables. Everything was either made of white plexiglass or titanium, and was very sterile looking. The office was comprised of one human and eight androids, all attired in white uniforms, and was strategically located for optimal visibility. All were doing various forms of work.

The Orionian then rose from his desk and spoke. "Isaac Glock, welcome to the Intergalactic Correctional Facility. I am sorry to hear of your breakdown. I am Dr. Michael Brewer. We will be diagnosing the computer chip in your brain and repairing any damage done to it. After completion, you will go before the Judicial Bureau at the Galactic Council to stand charges. First things first, however. You will be taken to our debriefing room where you will divulge the events of your last mission. Before we continue, we have to know what took place to disrupt your faculties."

I stood there quietly, not knowing what to expect next. I wondered, how did I get here? How long will I be here? Am I repairable? You see, physical illness and mental illness had been removed from our DNA years ago, as everyone had a computer chip installed upon birth. This chip was all inclusive and designed to "repair" any genetic defect inherited through the years. It basically lined up the genomes in the double helix molecule and eliminated any improprieties not suitable for stable human growth and compatibility. Now here I stood, an accomplished and respected Commander on the edge of being eradicated.

"Do you have any questions, Commander Glock?"

I stared at him, knowing anything I say may be detrimental. He too was tall and thin, with an accent from a northern galaxy.

"Yes, how long will I be here, and is my chip repairable?"

"Your length of stay may be long, as you have an advanced IQ, and many portals of your brain will have to be scanned. Whether we can line up your axions and dendrites in a suitable manner has to be determined. All chips are repairable, as it is a chip. Whether it fits your current DNA traits is another matter. If there is nothing else, please follow the android to the debriefing room."

"Yes Sir."

We then walked down another hallway that led to the next stage of my incarceration, the debriefing room. The decor was in stark contrast to the dayroom and office I just left. As the dayroom was bright and sterile looking, the debriefing room was soft looking with a pastel decor and comfortable furniture. One thing that didn't look comfortable was the recliner with wires attached to it that I was supposed to sit in.

Six panelists sat at a desk and overlooked the "chair." They introduced themselves as Fleet Commander Davolio, Galactic Judge Lisko, Psychiatrist Gilmore, Military Adjunct Ross, Galactic Theologian Peloza Augustine and Science Officer Novacich. All six were influential and experienced officers from our galaxy.

"Can I get you something before we start, Commander?" asked the technician.

"Some coffee from Orion would be nice," I said.

Orion was the major star group in our area and had several planets that revolved around it, one of which was used exclusively for harvesting the major food groups.

Chapter Two
Interrogation

Commander Isaac Glock was a highly regarded stellar officer of the Fleet, the highest commanding officer in that galactic segment. He was the son of a former stellar officer and had been meticulously trained for this assignment through the years. After many years of scientific and military training, essentially starting out as a plebe, he rapidly promoted to the rank of stellar officer in thirty-one short years. He has been the stellar officer for two years now. He was very intelligent and stood seven feet three inches. He was thinly built and was 67 years old. A breakdown to someone of his caliber was highly unusual.

The coffee was delivered by a female android that was made in our image, another attempt to make me feel more comfortable. As I sat there, I perused the room and the large hologram screen that filled one wall. It was a medical and psychological screen designed to detect any abnormalities in my brain. After my coffee and the subsequent hooking up to the wires, we commenced.

Judge Lisko began, "Commander, can you please recount the events that transpired during your last mission, the mission that brought you here? Please be specific, and may I remind you, any discrepancy from the truth will set off an electrical impulse notifying us of that fact. As you speak, you may be interrupted by a member on the panel that is educated in the area you're speaking of at the time. You can begin."

"First of all, I want to say our mission was one of education and peace, as the inhabitants of the Milky Way's Number Three were very primitive compared to us. Their galaxy is approximately 900 light years from our own. Our fleet was large, consisting of 200 huge mother ships with each to be positioned over each country on the planet and two for the country they call America. "

"Excuse me Commander, if your mission was one of peace, why such a large armada," inquired Ross?

"Sir, although primitive in their thinking, they do possess nuclear weapons."

"Go on."

"Each ship contained 1500 inhabitants, 1000 clones and 300 small vehicles for exploring and transporting, each robotically controlled. Each mother ship also contained 1,000 saucer shaped drones for defense and, if need be, military operations. From the ground, as you know, the mother ships are one-mile wide and very imposing, as they could be seen for miles as they loom overhead.

Our trip was long and took us through two separate wormholes, each one bringing us closer and quicker to our destination. There are many planets in the universe that support life as we know it, approximately 20 million to be exact, and Number Three has long been in our history books as we have visited them many times. It has also long been an experimental laboratory for our scientists, mainly because it is a planet similar to ours and a place to study violence at a distance safely removed from us.

Science Officer Novacich then asked, "Commander, are you saying that we have meddled in their history and development?"

"Yes, for thousands of years. We have also altered their DNA and cerebral size."

Everyone looked at him while they took notes.

"Can I continue?"

"You may."

"To give you a history, the temperature on Number Three varies greatly from -75 degrees to +140 degrees Fahrenheit, which is very different from our own planet. We have no ice caps, which gives us a median temperature of 72 degrees all year long. Our gravity index is similar to the gravity found on Number Three, which made us easier to navigate once we got there. There is also a large body of water on Number Three that occupies three fourths of the surface and has allowed us total freedom in the past. We have been able to enter their vast oceans at will, and remain undetectable to their inhabitants with underwater bases. The planet is also composed of life sustaining air, such as ours. Number Three has a circumference of 25,000 miles, whereas our planet has a circumference of 53,000 miles. The backside of the Moon on Number Three has been used as a base by us too, mainly because it doesn't rotate and was never visible to Number Three's occupants. It essentially shows the same side of the surface to the planet at all times. The Moon on Number Three has hollow pockets which go deep in to the Moon's core, which is hollow, and has allowed us to come and go whenever we wanted without being seen. The core also protects us from the extreme temperature difference between day and night and the random strikes of meteorites while we are based on the Moon, as the pockmarked surface shows a violent past.

Thousands of years ago, we mined and inhabited their planet in secluded areas but find that hard to do now, as they have increased dramatically in population and have acquired technical means to detect us. In the past, we also used them as slaves to do our mining and interbred with them to enhance their genetic structure. The rare minerals on Number Three, notably gold, platinum, and uranium, are very essential to our space craft and their nuclear capabilities, as well as electromagnetism, which we use to defy gravity and increase our speed. The main mining on their Moon consisted of Helium-3, a rare isotope in space that is used in nuclear fission and is also of prime importance to space travel.

We have watched the steady advances in science the Earthlings have made, and have within the past 225 years developed radio waves which are broadcast throughout the universe. It is through the waves they emit that their progress has been tracked. The increased hostility we have detected in the past fifty years and the nuclear tipped lasers they have incorporated into their satellites is the purpose of our journey. We have watched them go to their Moon and beyond. We had even made ourselves visible to them in space and in areas on their planet, but they are babies in universal time and frighten easily. Frankly, they do not appear ready for intervention at this time. Their Solar System is over 4 billion years old, whereas ours is 6 billion years old. Even though they have been here for a while, their ability to learn is hampered by their small cerebrum. Whereas their skull is round, our skull is elongated and has a much larger brain and memory capacity. Their progress in the sciences has been slow, and they have had to be brought along cautiously due their violent nature."

Galactic Theologian Augustine stopped him, "Commander Glock, if you felt they were not ready for intervention, why such a large armada? Why inflict psychological harm to a fragile species?"

"Ma'am, though they are infants cerebrally, they are quite hostile."

"Can you explain?"

"Yes, it is of recent events that brought us back at this time. Our earth-based androids have informed us they have developed a uranium-fissured bomb that can utterly destroy themselves and their planet and a means to of transport to deliver them. They have also begun visiting other planets in their own Solar System and began mining minerals on their Moon. Because of this, we can no longer use the back side of their Moon as a base. They are a warring people and essentially, we feel our genetic experiments with them have failed and that they may soon become a threat to others in the universe. Though violence is no longer in our DNA, if the inhabitants of Number Three do not agree to disarm their nuclear warheads, we will have to eliminate the warheads ourselves. Though they may see things differently, we have come with peaceful intentions.

CHAPTER THREE
History

Science Officer Novacich spoke, "Commander, Glock, do you feel your judgement was swayed by the past history of Earth and its inhabitants?"

"I don't believe so. I did try to stress to my crew their weaknesses and strengths, however."

"Okay, you can continue."

"For my mission to make an impact on you, I find it necessary to describe our ships' strengths and weaknesses. Our mother ships are essentially small cities comprised of approximately 3,000 people. They have all the conveniences for interstellar travel, living quarters, an aero-port, a laboratory, as well as a nucleus of scientists. They are shaped like a huge cartwheel with the perimeter always spinning at a slow rate of speed. In this way, we can gather all important radio waves and solar energy but most important of all, we create artificial gravity from the spin of our cartwheel. Each ship has a nuclear engine that is located in the aft of the hub with lead shields to protect the crew from neutrons, X-rays, and gamma rays the engine emits. It is fusion powered by Helium-3, a rare element that only could be mined on Saturn, Jupiter, and the Earth's oceans in this Solar System. Because of this super fuel, warp drive is attained, and speeds close to the speed of light are capable when traveling through a black hole. Because of the long distances travelled, it is not unusual to have generations of astronauts dwelling on the ship, as well as crew members frozen in time, only to be awakened when necessary.

The universe is divided into four quadrants but is forever expanding, with the Milky Way, as the inhabitants of Number Three call it, being among the closest Solar System to our own. As I ate dinner one night with Adam, the captain of our ship, I stared out the giant glass porthole and gazed at the oncoming stars as we travelled. I wondered what we may expect when we arrived, as we were going to have to make contact with the Earthlings this time. Their war machines are developed to the extent they can destroy most anything they know of and are dispersed throughout the planet. However, the physical and scientific makeup of their war machines are still very primitive compared to ours. Though they have developed stealth aircraft, we can make our huge mother ship disappear completely on their radar and we can repel their weapons with a protective shield which we control electromagnetically with dark matter. What we are most concerned about, and we discussed in length, was the saucer shaped space craft that they reverse engineered from a space craft we lost in 1947 and 2020 of their years. They went down in what they call Roswell, New Mexico, and the Sahara Desert, respectively. They carried advanced weapons, too advanced for their times and brain capacity. They simply can't reverse engineer the weapons that were onboard because they aren't knowledgeable in "dark matter" yet. But we have learned from our androids that the United States has a fleet of saucers now, even though they have actually denied their existence for years. My main concern is if they carry nuclear war tips, as the saucers are as maneuverable as ours.

Number Three, or Earth as they call it, has been a dumping ground for thousands of years of the uneducated misfits and criminals who occupied other similar planets, so the biological gene for violence has been instilled in all of them."

Psychiatrist Gilmore spoke, "Commander, are you saying we not only altered their DNA, but we also used Earth as a dumping ground for prisoners and derelicts in the past?"

"Yes Ma'am, not only us, but other factions and races have too. Earth is like no other. It is not pure, but a conglomeration of races and misfits."

"Go on."

"Any advanced education they may have had when they were deposited there had apparently been lost through time amid the many natural catastrophes that occur on Number Three. The planet is in constant turmoil, with wars, earthquakes, tornados, hurricanes, volcanoes, arid deserts and freezing tundra constantly changing the climate and terrain. Essentially, because of the turbulent weather and gravitational pull on the planet, it wants to be flat, constantly eroding and changing. The inhabitants were originally scattered among four large land masses and were of different color, language, and race. Each race was disposed by different aliens from other planets, the Blacks, the

Browns, and the Yellows. Each dwelled in an area where the weather was similar to the planet they came from. Our race was called Whites and we originally settled in an area they call the Mediterranean and Europe. Other aliens have visited here also, but because of their physical makeup and chemistry, they found the planet to be inhospitable, notably the Grays and the Reptilians. This planet was the home of an interbreeding experiment to check cerebral development over periods of time and to see whether their violent characteristics would grow or be diminished, thus the "missing link" the scientists of Number Three still search. In essence, we are their missing link, originally artificially crossbreeding with the Earthlings approximately 400,000 years ago, bringing their brain mass larger and accelerating them from cave man status. This planet originally held the lowest of man species and was crossbred by us over periods of time to enrich their environment and sociological makeup, as they were no more than erect apes.

Violence had been removed from our own biological makeup years ago, as it contributed to an unhealthy existence with many problems that trickled down to all phases of society. It also created much warfare in our past which was a huge detriment to growth and understanding. All aliens with the capacity of interstellar travel had previously visited this planet for thousands of years and watched the development of their own species, namely the Yellows and the Browns. They often fought over the planet Earth to keep a balance of power, as the violent gene has not been removed from their DNA. They are our biggest threat, and Number Three's inhabitants would have grown much more slowly than they have if it wasn't for our intervention."

CHAPTER FOUR
Earth's Geography

"When we first arrived, the Earthlings looked upon us as gods, mainly because of their lack of education and wisdom. The Greeks called us Titans and our past visitors were revered as gods, namely Zeus and Poseidon. We interbred with the Earthlings, in essence to build a super race. They had brawn and were physically imposing, while we had brains that were millions of years more developed than their brains. The Browns helped the Egyptians build large monuments to honor them, namely the three pyramids that mimic our own star system in the Orion Belt, as they too came from our star system.

Number Three's physical makeup consists of a violent core with moving masses of magma beneath the surface. The seismic energy results in an ever-changing geological view, with the shorelines constantly shifting and the mountains rising. On the surface, it can be quite volatile too as the weather there constantly changes. The large amount of water on the surface accounts for great temperature extremes as air is heated and then cooled, thus creating large variances in wind velocity. We also discovered a long time ago that there is an electromagnetic field that crisscrosses the planet, caused by the hot moving magma beneath the surface. Beneath some of these magnetic fields sits large aquifers. The magnetic field, in conjunction with the aquifers produces an electric field that can be harnessed and controlled. Present day Earthlings are aware of this energy and do not know how to harness this power, but the Browns used this energy to build the pyramids and large monuments 3,000 years ago that still exist in present day Egypt. It is on these areas where the pyramids are built that the aquifers and magnetic fields combine, allowing gravity-defying building and movement of large rocks to take place. The three large pyramids of Giza were subsequently arranged and aligned to mimic the three large stars in our Solar System, the Orion Belt. This electromagnetic force not only allowed for the movement of large stone blocks but also gave them the energy to power their space craft when they left.

On one of our many visits to Earth thousands of years ago, we first developed a base at the most northern part of their sphere, on their pole. The temperature there was moderate at the time. But through the years, their planet turned cold and the poles became ice caps, covering the most northern and southern ends of the orb. When it did so, the water level dramatically decreased, exposing new shorelines. We then moved our base and occupied an area on a beautiful island in the middle of a large water expanse. We called it Atlantis. The island was large and located off the coast of two large continents, Europe and the one the Earthlings call Africa, the same continent that the Blacks and Browns occupied. The main city was shaped like a large cartwheel, mimicking our mother ships, with the center being the hub. The science officers dwelt there among many laboratories and a large observatory to teach astronomy to the Atlantians. We had lived there helping the inhabitants of this planet for approximately 3,000 of their years, giving them a vast knowledge of science, mathematics and astronomy. It seemed their life expectancy only existed of about forty years at the time of our arrival. But with our interbreeding, their life expectancy actually increased dramatically to 800 900 years, with the last of their descendants, a man they called Moses, actually almost living to the age of 900 of their years. They had no way to measure time, so we gave them a calendar, along with ways to follow it and diagrams to chart the stars.

The people were illiterate when we arrived, as were others that were scattered all over the planet. Their planet was actually a laboratory to us, watching and helping the progress of their civilization. Our colony at this time was only confined to Atlantis, experimenting and enriching the lives of these people only, but later on we held bases in the Easter Islands, Central America, and the Nazca Plains in South America. They all built monuments to honor us, as again they looked at us as gods. While we occupied and mined earth at that time, nomadic tribes had crossed the continents through exposed land bridges and started crossbreeding with each other. However, this crossbreeding only led to a more violent race as people with the violent gene bred with the non-violent people. This only hindered and slowed their cerebral growth as more warfare developed and only the strongest of the specie survived. Because of their accelerated brain growth, they simply found new ways to master the elements of war.

Eventually, the ice caps began to melt, which we learned was a cyclical event that occurred on Earth about every 26,000 years. This melting of the caps then covered the exposed land bridges and along with a cataclysmic earthquake, Atlantis was completely inundated, thus erasing all the good we had accomplished through the years. The flooding on the planet was gradual, but the sudden quake sunk the island and killed everyone, including our technicians and scientists, leaving the island totally destroyed and submerged under a bed of lava in the Atlantic Ocean.

Much of Number Three's history has been lost through the years, mainly because of the planet's violent and ever-changing environment and the fact that every 26,000 years the planet's poles freeze and their ice advances towards their equator, erasing everything in the process, and then gradually melts. This cycle removes and wipes out many cultures that dwelled on the continents and near the coastlines. Because of periodic droughts, the people of Easter Island and the Nazca Plains also became extinct. The Mayans, however, were a pure breed and learned our ways quickly, developing a calendar that could accurately predict astronomical events for thousands of years, including the death cycle of Earth's inhabitants.

Chapter Five
The Journey

Commander Davolio spoke, "Commander Glock, it appears you have great knowledge of Earth's history. Was this passed on to your captains and their starship crews?"

I couldn't help but look at the wall hologram while she spoke, every facet of my physiological makeup was being illustrated.

"Yes Ma'am, they were educated extensively regarding their history, strengths and weaknesses."

"Was your trip uneventful or did you encumber any technical problems?"

"It was a rough trip, Commander Davolio. Adam, excuse me, Captain Adam Schutz and I couldn't help but think about the last wormhole we traversed, with the internal force of the wormhole almost tearing our spaceship apart. We had to use our electromagnetic and dark matter capabilities to ensure the wormholes opening was open long enough for us to go from the mouth of the wormhole to the mouth at its conclusion.

This was done by creating exotic matter, essentially creating a negative energy density and a larger negative pressure than the density of the wormhole, thus allowing us to pass through the tunnel at sub-light speeds, approximately 180,000 mile per second and slightly under the speed of light. Even a mistake of a few photons could disrupt the journey through the wormhole, either by destroying our ship, or dispensing you at a point in space far from your intended destination.

Our dining room was large and we are served by robots built in our image, the same robots that actually occupy Earth as we speak. They are androids and are physically indistinguishable from us, doing our menial work as well as our technical work. They have an internal headband that sees and records everything we do, say, and think, and can be readily read and downloaded by system control on every mother ship at any time. While our computer chip is compatible with our DNA, theirs is built internally to make it invisible and to comply with their daily functions. The chip serves as our identification, as a Social Security card once identified the people of Earth, but is instantaneously recognizable by any scanner on any ship. Some androids have been groomed to hold important government positions in important countries on Earth, positions that will sway to our position and be ready when called upon. Others have been groomed as scientists to further their growth, albeit slowly, as they are too violent to absorb scientific principles quickly. All of our food and water is produced on our ship, while any necessary minerals we may need for space fuel can be picked up at various moons and planets along the way. We were able to convert them to energy as we needed it.

Adam and I walked the hanger and discussed the many journeys our people have made to this planet, and the many battles we have had with other warfaring aliens trying to maintain peace there. Our star system is one of the Orion Belt stars that can be seen from Earth without a telescope. Our planet, Hercules, rotates around the double star system Mintaka, and is 915 light years from Earth. The pyramids, in what the Earthlings now call Egypt, assimilated our location in the heavens and were built by the Browns, who lived in our star vicinity. We discussed this in large detail and how their forefathers tried to teach the Egyptians hieroglyphics and how the language was lost through the years. It seems because of the many catastrophes that happen on Earth, you can say that Earth's history has suffered from amnesia. All of their previous cultures have simply been erased through cataclysmic events.

After coming out of the wormhole, we were in a position to see the entire Solar System of Number Three and the planet they call Earth. We soon entered their Solar System and had to be on guard for the aliens responsible for creating the "Evil Axis," which now threatens the peace on this planet. They too have intermingled with the Earthlings and have been there for years, actually living and assimilating with them as our androids have done. They have tried to rebuff our presence before, but through the years we have managed to stay ahead of them technologically, passing on our expertise to the United States gradually through inadvertent means, with our insignificant androids working in strategic locations making "scientific breakthroughs" periodically to help them along. We have chosen the United States because they appear to be the strongest faction on the planet and are direct descendants of the European people we bred within the past.

Earth's Solar System is composed of eight large planets and four outer dwarf planets, all on an elliptical plane circling their star which they call the "Sun." In addition to thousands of small bodies in these regions, various other small bodies, such as comets, centaurs and interplanetary dust, travel freely between these regions and can be quite dangerous to space travel if not detected. This is an area called the Kuyper Belt and is composed mostly of ices such as water, ammonia, and methane. It is nine billion miles from the edge of their Solar System to Earth, and with us travelling at a speed of 500,000 miles per hour, it will take us eight months to get there.

When we finished the hanger inspection, we went to the bridge located in the center of the hub where we could visually see the entire Solar System at once as we entered it. The bridge was a large, round, silicon diamond-based glass room with hologram screens that gave a view of 360 degrees of our space ship with temperature, speed, and communication detectors scanning the cosmos. It was completely circular with a glass floor, and dimly lit with an aura of blue light coming from the computers' and hologram screens that were present in the room. As you stood or sat on the bridge, you had a beautiful view of the cosmos from every position as the ship transcended through the black, star-lit galaxy. Every facet of the huge mother ship was directed from the bridge, and each was manned by skilled technicians that have worked their way to this responsibility by years of experience in all locations and circumstances learned in the many difficult and unpredictable circumstances the universe could throw at them.

We slowed the speed of our crafts to 100,000 miles per hour to conserve energy and planned our final approach. We passed the large giant planets, composed mostly of gas, and were approaching the asteroid belt, which is composed mostly of rock and metal. After traversing this belt, we would pass Mars and then have Earth in plain view. Our forefathers actually had a base on Mars about a million years ago, when it was full of water and had an atmosphere consisting of oxygen, quite capable of sustaining the large population and civilization it had. The history of Mars went back a million years before man started walking the surface of Earth. After many volcanic catastrophes which spewed large quantities of iron ash, the atmosphere turned arid and dried up, the red iron dust eventually extinguished all life on the planet. When this happened, we actually moved our base and many of the inhabitants to Earth, where a primitive civilization was developed and subsequently ruined when one of many asteroids hit the planet Earth in the past. The planet Mars is now occasionally used by the Browns and their robots for mining. Much mining was done on Mars in the past, as it was rich in gold, iron, titanium and uranium. The Browns left their legacy there as they did in Egypt. On Mars they left a large mountain carved into a face, a face that is still visible to Earth and which has confused scientists on Earth for decades. Canals, which were used for transporting water in the final days of Mars drought, are still visible from Earth.

Chapter Six
Contact

"I was closer to Adam than other officers and we discussed the mission at length. We stared out of the large round porthole in the officers' quarters as we observed the thin blue line that enclosed the air space of Earth. It is this thin blue line that ensures life that can be sustained on Earth. It contains the oxygen and air needed for life, and protects the Earth from dangerous solar rays and radiation. It is one of the common denominators needed to support life. Of all the millions of planets that support human life, they have four things in common: water, air, a median temperature, and a thin blue line that protects the planet from solar radiation and random meteorites. The blue line is their atmosphere's reflection from the vast oceans that occupy their planet.

I looked at Captain Schultz, "Do you think they will be aggressive when we make ourselves known? Everything in their make-up leads to that."

Adam Schultz was a loyal Captain and I could not do without him. He essentially complimented me in every facet of our profession. He was tall of stature and was inherently bred from a long line of parents who specialized in space travel. He has been at my side for four of our years now and I will dread the time when he is promoted, although I will understand it completely. He simply will make a fine stellar officer.

"Only time will tell," he said. "We are cloaked at the moment. When do you want me to shut down their electronic devices and satellites?"

"I stared at the blue planet while I contemplated his question. I turned on the monitor, and the thousands of satellites that circled Earth lit up instantly. My communication officer said he has received reports that our presence was made known before we turned on our cloaking device. The Air Force of the United States activated their laser armed satellites, while the United States and Russian Air Forces were scrambling to get airborne. I was aware that I made our presence known, and I had done it intentionally so that the Americans and Russians in charge knew the magnitude of our presence and had time to think about it before we made contact. Both the United States and Russia have shot at our vehicles before, with one of our craft ultimately crashed in Roswell a hundred years ago, and in Siberia in 2020, but lately, in fear of retaliation, they just escort our crafts and push them out of their areas. Today would be different though. Our ship would be cloaked and theirs will be inoperable.

During our two-year trip to Earth, we developed a plan of engagement with my captains and disciplines of each mother ship in order to avoid a conflict of any kind. I repeat, our mission was one of education and peace, as we now feared their latest military advancement in space. Because of their warfaring characteristics, they are not only a danger to themselves, but are now a danger to all others in the Solar System. They had a history of firing at us before, about a hundred years ago, in the fifties and sixties, actually shooting down two of our saucers, one in America and one in Russia. They then reverse engineered the aircraft, leaving both countries with a fleet of saucers and pilots that are extremely aggressive and unpredictable. They will think our substantial presence is an invasion, so we must control each and every situation that develops. My biggest fear is that our impending visit will dramatically alter their religious belief system, and probably throw their theological world into chaos."

Galactic Theologian Peloza-Augustine then interrupted, "Commander, with your vast background in Earth Science, did you ever foresee what your visit would to their psyche?"

"I did Ma'am, but I was weighing the consequences of each problem we were facing. It seemed the misuse of nuclear power outweighed a belief system that could eventually be understood."

"Go on."

"Our plan of engagement was six-fold. First of all, we will disable all military and communication satellites that orbit their planet. They have just recently developed and constructed a floating nuclear Air Force base that contains saucers they built from copying our technology. They practically control the globe with this technology. They also have satellites that can shoot down aircraft with a laser beam, and these will be disabled first.

Second, we will disable all sources of electrical and nuclear power grids, basically rendering them inoperative. We will then immobilize the electronic devices on all airbases and naval vessels. This will bring them to their knees and render them helpless.

Third, we will uncloak our mother ships, making them visible to all. Americans call this ploy "Shock and Awe." We will then place one ship over the capital of each country on Earth and hover there. Each mother ship, along with their saucer drones, will be in control of the subjects and military in their own region.

Fourth, we will open communications with the leaders and scientists of each district, as well as the general population, through their own satellites. The scientists will be more responsive than the politicians and far more educated. By then, the population will know who we are and why we came. The scientists will be allowed to conduct interactions and communiqué with each mother ship. This is where our androids that hold important positions on Earth will come into play, as they have been aware of our coming for months. The population in general will eventually and hopefully dissolve some of their fears as they see we come in peace.

Fifth, after an exchange of ideas and dialog has taken place, we will send an unarmed drone to each area to pick up the delegates from each location. They will be brought up to each mother ship and transported to the main mother ship's assembly hall where dialogue will commence.

Sixth, after exposing ourselves and educating them on the history and principles of the universe, as well as their own planet, we will set up a plan of action for their further growth. This will include disarming nuclear warheads and teaching them new peaceful uses of nuclear power, as well as enlightening them on the benefits of world and stellar peace. New agricultural and energy technology will be taught, because essentially, the main reason for war is hunger, greed, and the demand for energy.

If there is a glitch of any kind, or if there is interference from our adversaries, namely the Browns, Blacks or Yellows, we will be forced to extinguish anyone opposing our peace plan. The planet has simply become too dangerous for the peace of the universe to allow them to continue down the path they chose."

Adjunct Ross spoke, "Commander, it appears your mind was already made up regarding the use of force."

"Sir, I think I described the importance of our trip. The mission was outlined to us by Galactic Control before we embarked."

"Are you saying you had permission to use deadly force?"

"Sir, what I am saying is we were sent to educate the Earthlings about the values of the Solar System and what they do has ramifications that span the heavens. We were sent there to disarm them and re-educate them."

Military Adjunct Ross looked at the wall, then looked at Commander Glock. "Commander, did you have a back-up plan? You put a lot on the line here, exposing yourself, exposing us to them. What if they couldn't handle this visit? You know you weren't going to occupy the planet. Did you ever wonder what their lives would be like after you left?"

The board went crazy reading the emotions of Glock. It literally lit up the room and turned everyone's head. Glock saw it too and didn't know if it was the anger he was feeling for being questioned in such a manner or whether there really was a defect in his chip.

"Sir, we considered everything and felt they were ready for contact. It was either that or face nuclear warheads in space. We felt we made the right decision."

"Continue Sir."

CHAPTER SEVEN
Entry

I then said, "Adam, disable all military and communication satellites. We are close enough for intervention."

"Yes Sir."

Before we entered the thin blue line that envelops their planet and went into stealth mode, we passed their space base without provocation. We then entered their atmosphere at free will, as their radar and defensive capabilities were disabled. Not only would we be invisible to their radar, the heat from our electromagnetic shield also produces a giant cumulous cloud that envelops our ship and follows us as we travel. In essence, the electromagnetic rays that our shields emit influences the atmosphere around us and creates clouds that hide us. Because of this effect it also creates its own weather around us, leaving us completely hidden from below and above.

I then stared at the monitor. "Adam, have all of the Captains on their respective ships shut down the source of power to the naval ships and aircraft in their respective areas, including their magnetos? Render their nuclear aircraft carriers inoperative, and bring their nuclear submarines to the surface."

"Yes sir. We have already disabled the military and communication satellites."

"Thank you, Adam. We will turn on their VHF satellites when we want to communicate with them. They'll be able to see and hear us on their holograms and computers when we're ready. Joshua, take us down to 25,000 feet and have our mother ships hover over each intended capital of the country to which they are assigned. Have them turn their power grids back on in their respective areas, and give me updates of the Earthlings' communication with each other. I want to know their plans and how they're responding to this attack."

My assistant commander, Joshua Stonecypher, has been with me for twenty years and is very capable, being schooled in nuclear science and plasma engineering. He is my second-in-command, and essentially has the authority to command all phases of this operation in case of my demise.

"Joshua, put us in an area over the White House in Washington D.C., and stage the other mother ship designated for America between their Area 51 and Colorado Springs, the new home of their saucer fleet and America's dark programs. We will control the other mother ships on the planet from Washington. Let me know when everyone is in place."

"Yes sir, Commander. Commander, we are receiving reports of a fleet of star ships headed this way. They are led by Muhammad Khartoum of the Browns and they just passed Uranus and are approximately ten earth days out, traveling at 300,000 miles per hour."

"How big is their contingent Joshua?"

"It appears to be huge, approximately 320 star ships. The Browns must have tapped into our communication system before we left. They're contingent is too strong and they are tailing us too close to be a random visit. It appears they don't want peace to exist on this planet and will deploy all means possible to stop us."

"Joshua, our forefathers have fought battles with them over this planet in the past. We fought a war over the country they call

India a couple of thousand years ago. The locals were so primitive, they referred to our ships as "flying carpets" and "dragons". Contact the captains of the other mother ships and tell them we are in "code brown". They will know what procedures to follow. Do the Browns still use their abandoned base on Mars?"

"No sir. They aborted that base a few years ago when the Americans established an outpost there and haven't been back since. Even though they were underground and the Americans were never aware of their presence, they felt their occupation was too close. They also abandoned their base on the back side of the Moon when the Americans landed there in the sixties. However, because of its proximity, that doesn't prevent them from establishing a home base there for this engagement now. Our physical presence has let the secret out of the bag. It won't matter that we'll be exposed to the public anymore."

"Well, we have our work cut out for us now. We only have nine days to establish a pact with the Earthlings. After that, because of the Browns' presence, anything can happen. It would be foolish to start a war here, especially since we came in peace. Of course, the magnitude of our weapons which would be displayed on the Browns would also emphasize why peace is so important. The Earthlings will be in awe of the immediate and final destruction we could cause."

Chapter Eight
The Meeting

Military Officer Ross then asked a question, "Commander, it appears you were ready to confront the Browns without any communication." Before I could speak, the wall lit up like the Fourth of July.

"Officer Ross, although the wall is going off, I must tell you we would never confront any adversary without an attempt at a negotiation."

"Did you have any prior history with Khartoum?"

"No Sir, but I was totally aware of his aggressive past behavior and I wanted to be prepared for anything."

"Go on Sir."

"I then had my ship, the Vesuvius, positioned over the White House and opened the communication system to the President. He and his junior officers sat at the round table while he spoke."

"Mr. President and fellow colleagues, this day will be a momentous time in Earth history. Today, you, and particularly the public, officially find out you are not alone in this universe. We are here because we have become aware of your intentions to bring nuclear warheads into space. We cannot and will not tolerate this. For the first time in your short existence, you have the opportunity to establish a long lasting peace, a peace that has evaded you since your beginning in time. We apologize for our abrupt silencing of your military and your communication abilities. We only did so to protect you, as we know of your violent nature. We are not here to invade you or inflict harm of any kind, but to educate you and your fellow beings on the history of the universe and how you can have a safe and rewarding existence in it. We have so much to share with you. In essence, your history books will be rewritten after our visit, and your theological ideas will change dramatically. We came to you and did not go to the United Nations, as we feel they have no real power. They have over politicized their existence and have shown they are useless for achieving and maintaining world peace. However, as we speak, we have a mother ship positioned over every country's capital city in the world so that dialogue can commence. For your information, we also have a ship positioned over an area covering the border of Nevada and Colorado where you hide your fleet of saucers, and conduct your black projects. Yes, we know about them, and now everyone else does. I am Commander Glock, and my staff is here to answer any questions you may have. I do suggest that you quickly summon the best scientists in your country, from every discipline, in order to have more effective dialogue and communications. They will have many questions of which you politicians would never think of."

"Commander Glock, this is President Martinez. My domestic and military staff is present and we have you on our wall. It would be remiss of me if I didn't say we are unprotected and unable to provide an adequate defense against an attack. We have never been helpless before, so forgive me if I almost sound apologetic. I understand the purpose of your mission, but we are in a nuclear arms race here. If we don't keep it up we will render ourselves helpless and subservient to our foes. This world has changed dramatically in the last one hundred years, but today's events are staggering, to say the least. Why, What, How? I don't know where to start."

"President Martinez, I repeat to you that we are not here to attack, but you act surprised at our presence. You have been aware of an alien existence for years, ever since you shot down one of our saucer probes a hundred years ago at Roswell and kept it from the public. Your adversary, Russia, has also shot down one of our spacecraft. I'm sure you have communicated with them about it. We also know you have reverse engineered the saucer and now command a large fleet of them. So please, spare me your humility."

"Commander Glock, it will take a couple of days to assemble our scientists. As you know, they are scattered all over the country, as well as some in Europe and Asia. With the power grids and airline communication down, how do you expect me to assemble them?"

"President Martinez, you contact me here when you have their location and I will allow those scientists to fly to Washington, and only those planes will be allowed airborne. Your scientists that are out of the country will be flown to the capital of the country they are in and transported here by us. Our monitor will be open to yours on a 24-hour basis. You will be dealing with my assistant commander, Joshua. He will convey your information to me. Once everyone is assembled, the scientists of the world will be shuttled to Washington and I will return to the table. Time is of the essence, as a problem has developed, a problem that can't be relayed to you at this time, but I can assure you that if it isn't handled properly, it can change the course of events in the immediate future."

"Commander Glock, what about the power grids? What about the people who rely on power for food and their health?"

"Power will be turned on to the people; however, all power to military bases and naval ships will cease to function. Our electromagnetic anti-gravity devices will not allow anything to function there, not even with your auxiliary power. We have landed your planes, stopped your ships, had your nuclear submarines surfaced, shut down your satellites, and disarmed your missiles. You need not worry about your adversaries, as their military bases and hardware are shut down too. This visit isn't just to America. We are also communicating with your allies and adversaries as we speak. They too are assembling their scientists. When this is completed, a meeting of the world will take place, a real meeting, a meeting that will make your grandiose United Nations look like a nursery school. Are there any other questions?"

"No sir."

"Remember, President Martinez, time is of the essence."

The hologram was turned off, and an overtly dazed President Martinez stood up and looked at his staff. They were all talking at the same time, some to each other, some trying to get President Martinez's attention.

"Please, please, let's calm down. John, assemble our best scientists and their location so that they can be brought here immediately. General Wright, relay a message to every military base through Commander Glock, and tell them to stand by, and tell them what has transpired. I also want you to assemble every general in D.C. and come up with an alternative plan of action. Paul, mass hysteria could develop if we don't handle this carefully. Although the public has flirted with the idea of an alien existence, it has never been acknowledged, even though we have primed the public gradually with informative historical programs on the networks for years. Set up the networks for me, and prepare a speech for me. I must address the union. I want each and every one of you to consult your staff. We must be calm. History is changing before us by leaps and bounds, and we must have a steady hand."

Chapter Nine
Shock and Awe

"There is a lot to digest here Commander," said Commander Davolio, with Officer Ross nodding his head. "This was a very aggressive strategy you employed. Did you consider the health and welfare of the people?"

"Yes Ma'am, we made sure the populace wasn't deprived of life sustaining properties. I have to believe we covered all bases, as we knew their warlike tendencies. We felt we had to be aggressive to get their attention. "

"I see," said Judge Lisko, as she perused the hologram. "Commander, it appears to me you were interfering with their belief system, couldn't there have been another way to achieve your goal?"

"Look, Ladies and Gentleman, I'm quite sure there could have been as many ways to confront this as there are commanders' opinions. This is the route we chose."

"Please continue Sir."

"I then gave the order for each mother ship to descend to twelve thousand feet and to make their physical presence known over their respected areas. Twelve thousand feet was a good altitude because the ships could loom larger and be seen by more people on their own horizon. The sheer size of each ship will amaze the inhabitants of each country and cause fear and panic. In doing so, their cloaking ability will be turned off, and all of the military might of the Earthlings will have been rendered helpless and inoperative by then."

As the ship became visible over Washington D.C., the bureaucrats stared out of their windows in disbelief. The freeways that left town were crowded with confused and panicked people, each wanting to leave and each not knowing where to go. The lines of communication were allowed to be open and the lines to the White House were jammed with calls, each one with a different agenda. The heads of state and cabinet members had their families whisked underground to a bunker under the Capital Building that had been built in the nineteen fifties. Since the fifties, the bunker had eventually grown, stretched with a tunnel that actually went from D.C. to the Norad installation in the mountains of Colorado, with two bullet train tracks that fed the system. This was top secret and only known to members of the CIA, NSA, the President, Cabinet and leaders of the House, with instructions to be made known to other staff members in an emergency. Meanwhile, the people of America became frantic. Joe the cab driver called his family and told them to pack and get ready to leave. They were going to the country. Sam, a survivalist, grabbed his family and headed for an abandoned nuclear missile silo in Kansas he had purchased from the government, just in case something like this happened. In New York, Father Mackenzie called Rabbi Steinberg and arranged for an unheard-of meeting between the two of them. In Rome, the Vatican was swamped with visitors, and at the Wailing Wall, people wept. It seems people were flocking to their source of congregation, and there wasn't enough room to accommodate them all. In addition, they had to put out a message to the people that completely contradicted everything they've been taught through the years and didn't know where to start.

As a mother ship was En route to Area 51 in the Nevada desert, it stopped over the Hoover Dam and drained it of its electromagnetic power, thus resupplying its ship with vital energy. The newly named capital of the new state, Las Vegas, South Nevada, subsequently went dark, as well as the cease of functioning of all slot machines and gaming activities. The mother ship then flew over the area, leaving the residents on the street of the strip shocked and bewildered. All vehicles were stopped in their paths while the ship glided over at 12,000 feet, illuminating the large casinos with an incandescent eerie glow, and leaving a giant reflection in the pool of the newly built Star Wars Casino. It stopped over the third pyramid of the Luxor and reflected off its glass walls, creating an image that may have existed thousands of years ago in Egypt. It was the first time that Las Vegas had been shut down and security in the casinos scrambled to protect their interests from marauding citizens and tourists.

As the other mother ships took their place over the world's capitals, mass hysteria developed. In the Vatican, Saint Peter's Square was being overrun with bewildered

Catholics. In Kabul, Cairo, Beijing, and all of the 51 other capitals that declared Islam their number one religion, uncertainty followed, as well as the countries that prayed to Buddha. As a mother ship hovered over Jerusalem, people at the Wailing Wall stopped praying and got up off their knees and stared upwards in disbelief. People all over the world were dying from heart attacks and mesmerized in fear. Nuclear submarines were forced to come to the surface and the nuclear planes and drones of the Air Forces of the world were grounded. Missile silos were inoperative as well as communication between military bases. Military and commercial satellites stopped functioning, as chaos and confusion circled the globe.

As I watched the mass hysteria take place, I turned to Joshua. "Because of the many cataclysmic events and years of warfare on this planet, these people have no semblance of reality without their religion. Wait until they find out that the gods they were worshipping are actually ancestors of the Browns, Yellows, and Whites who visited their planet thousands of years ago!"

"Commander, how long are you going to let this go on? How long will the satellites be closed for communication?"

"Joshua, we have to bring them to their knees first. They have to be humbled. Because of their inadequate education, they have been living in a vacuum, a fairytale existence portrayed by their government for years.

When computers, robots and drones replaced the working man in the middle of their 21st century, their social progress regressed to their middle ages. Mass unemployment led to the walking poor and large amounts of homeless that the government couldn't sustain. People lived in communities in the deserts and lit the night with camp fires. It is a barbaric existence with food being meager and education being non-existent out of the metropolitan areas. This created hunger and hunger creates wars. Their militaries are strong because of this. They have been trying to repel a revolution for years. We must also talk to their scientists before we have any dialogue with the masses. Then in conjunction with their scientists, we will sit down and give them a history lesson of planet Earth. They have to know that they are not alone in this Universe and not as almighty as they think they are. Then and only then will we make progress."

"Yes Commander, the government has been hiding out existence from the public for over one hundred years and their theological beliefs have been embedded in their brains for eons. That accounts for part of the mass hysteria we are watching. I can only wonder how their mental psyche is disturbed at our visit."

"This is disturbing, Joshua! They have been killing each other in the name of God ever since we first appeared here thousands of years ago. In what they call the Middle East, the Browns had armed their people and converged on the country they call Israel, attacking from all sides in 2020. They created a boiling brew of unbelievable fanaticism and hate that continues to this day. Our androids in America and Israel were influential in protecting them and eventually disabled their military in 2021, thus enabling Israel to expand their borders to include part of Egypt, Iraq, and Jordan. After all, the Europeans, Israelis and Americans are all descendants of ours and we have always protected them."

As they spoke, scientists from all over the globe converged on their respective countries for their transport to the mother ships. Churches were filled and the questions started: "Who are they? Why are they here? Where did they come from? What do they want? Has Jesus returned? Has Muhammad returned? Is this the end of times? Is this Armageddon? Where is our military? Why haven't they responded?" Billions of people looked at it in billions of ways. There were as many questions as there are people.

As these events took place, darkness fell on the planet in Europe and Africa first. For the first time on Earth the cat was out of the bag, and people looked to the skies and knew they were not alone. The mother ships, more than a mile wide, were aglow with an orangey-yellow eerie color, a color that transcended into fear for everyone who watched. It glowed through the windows of their homes with a fiery glow, a glow that sent children watching in amazement and parents reeling in fear, thinking that this was indeed hell, and Satan himself was visiting them. Theologians had no answers for their parishioners. They simply would have to watch and wait. Everyone knew a meeting was coming up with scientists who were summoned. Their holograms on their living room walls told them so. Energy was returned to the people so they could watch what was happening and not for philanthropic reasons, as all entertainment satellites were cut off. I knew that mass hysteria would take place, and this was one way of controlling the situation. For peace to happen, the masses would have to join together and put pressure on their respective governments for change. It would have to come from within.

But what was happening on the ground was child's play compared to what could happen in the skies above. But I had bigger fish to fry.

"Joshua, open our channels with Muhammad Khartoum's fleet. Let's eavesdrop on them. Perhaps we can detect what their plans are and where they intend to attack. You know, they have brought ill will to this planet and other planets for centuries. Their people in the Middle East started a terrorist campaign a couple of centuries ago against the western world, and have turned their religion into a zealous aberration, essentially brain washing the young and killing in the name of Allah. It continues to this day."

"Commander, I propose that we would be far more superior to them in space than here. Our weapons would be far more effective too. Don't you think we should send half our fleet out to intercept them? We could cloak them and wait for them on the backside of Mars. It would be a complete surprise. Of the two hundred countries on Earth, there are only six large armies: The United States of America, the United States of Europe, Russia, China, India and the United Republic of North Africa, with each country in their respective area buying their safety. Only one hundred of them have scientists we are interested in. We could send up the one hundred ships where a military is absent and where scientists are scarce and leave one hundred ships here. The countries we are leaving have already been exposed to our might, and the psychological effect the ships carried has already been established there."

I then walked to the wall and touched the hologram screen and was in instant contact with the mother ships he wanted to move. He went to a secluded channel that had a frequency the Browns couldn't detect.

"Attention all Captains, I want each of you to withdraw and proceed to Mars immediately. You are in Code Brown, DEFCON 3. I want you to travel the entire distance cloaked, and stay cloaked, until you hear otherwise. Communicate only on this channel. I will be in touch with you soon."

In the poor and impoverished countries that the mother ships abandoned, people prayed and chanted while looking to the skies and feared their return. They looked at the prehistoric drawings on the walls of their caves that their ancestors drew, and knew that the gods have returned.

CHAPTER TEN
The Browns

Dr. Gilmore glanced at the wall and then looked at her notes, "Commander, without having been to Earth in a while, you sure took a lot for granted regarding their mental psyche. You could have caused irreparable damage with your 'shock and awe' technique."

"Dr. Gilmore, this tactic has been used for years in many military campaigns and has always proved effective."

"Commander, this was not to be a military campaign, as you have stated many times already. Your escalation could have been disastrous."

"Ma'am, I did what I thought was necessary. Khartoum was on my back and we had no time to be nice."

"Very well, your comments will be taken into account. Continue Commander."

"I then returned to the round table and conferred with my staff regarding the impending confrontation with the Browns.

The star ships that the Browns employed was inferior to the mother ships I commanded, and everyone knew it. Although the Browns had learned to control exotic matter, their knowledge of black matter was only confined to space travel and not weapon development. They could maneuver through worm holes, but didn't have the long-range capabilities our weapons have. We could actually bend space and create a worm hole for our laser to travel through, essentially destroying them at long distance. They wouldn't know what hit them because we wouldn't be on their horizon."

Science Officer Novacich then replied, "Commander, how could you be sure that the Brown's hadn't perfected their use of black matter?"

"Sir, we are updated weekly regarding their nuclear and physics advances. We have clones integrated into their scientific community and they report to us weekly."

"Continue Sir, I am curious to see what took place."

I then asked my assistant commander, "Joshua, what class Star Ship is heading our way? Is it the SS4000 or their latest version, the SS5000?"

The SS4000 was approximately three fourths of a mile across and was engineered years ago, while the SS5000 was their latest attempt at catching up to the Whites technology. The SS5000 was a little over a mile across and carried 500 more personnel than the SS4000, with 200 more military craft than their mother ships. What they couldn't do technologically, they tried to make up with numbers. The star ships have a nuclear reactor for propulsion, but also rely on sails to collect photons from the stars. The lasers pointed on the sails convert them to energy that help propel their ships through space. Their ships are wedge-shaped with their sails set up behind them, which are actually made of gold foil and a mile wider than their craft. While our mother ships are set up for scientific purposes and defense, their ships are made for mining and military use only. Muhammad Khartoum has been their Commander for seventy years now and is quite capable; however, he has never gone up against the latest model mother ship and may not even know of its latest deadly capabilities. It will take four days for our mother ships to reach Mars, leaving them a day and a half to set up for their confrontation with Khartoum, if necessary.

"Commander, it is a combination of the SS4000 and the SS5000 flying in a giant wedge formation. Breaking them down, it is one hundred SS4000's and two hundred and twenty SS5000's, with Commander Khartoum's craft concealed in the rear and to the center of the formation. They will outnumber our saucers by two to one."

"Yes, but we will have a tactical advantage in our ambush. They may never be able to launch them if it goes as I plan. Adam, do all of our saucers have the new dark matter laser on board?"

"Yes Sir. They have the capability of destroying their craft at a distance, even if they are cloaked. That is our advantage. However, we will have to make ourselves visible for the split second that we fire. It won't matter, though… a millisecond leaves them no time to respond."

"That's correct Joshua, if we are all synchronized with our nuclear clock when we fire. Otherwise, our location will be visible to them as we fire. Okay, get

Commander Khartoum on the wall. Maybe we can avert this."

"Yes Sir. The initial delay will take 90 minutes. After that you can converse together."

"Thank you. Have my military officers and Head of Galactic Affairs summoned here for the meeting."

"Yes Sir. Commander, we are receiving communication from our ships in Europe and Asia. It seems the scientists will be ready to be shuttled here in four hours. The scientists in America will be ready in five hours, but we are having trouble assembling the scientists in North Africa. There is still a war being fought there."

"Joshua, when they board our ship, have them walk through a truth analyzer. I want their cortex scanned as they answer questions. Each scientist must be able to answer questions regarding his or her specific science. I don't want any double agents on this ship. Since they don't have a microchip embedded in them, have their corneas scanned in case they have to return. That will be their identity."

"Captain Schultz, are you prepared for shuttle arrivals? It appears that it will only be several hours away. Upon entering our ship, I want the scientists to walk past our galactic observatory on the way to the assembly hall. Leave a hangar door open. I would also like them to casually get a glimpse of our battalion of saucers and drones as they walk here. I want them profoundly impressed, and I want them scared. Any psychological advantage will work in our favor. We will show them where they belong in the cosmos scheme of things."

"Yes Commander, I will be in contact with the respective captains and coordinate the shuttle arrivals. I think the mere size of our ship will awe them, not to mention the technology we can display."

"General Heinz, we have a full plate here. In respect to code Brown, I want a plan of attack in case dialogue with Khartoum is futile. With respect to destroying the future military capability of the armies on this planet, I would like a sociological and psychological report as to whether this is feasible at this time. Are they really ready for a lasting peace, or is it possible that they still have primitive tendencies and aren't cerebrally developed enough at this time to comprehend a peaceful future?"

"Commander, there's more at play here. Economics and land grabbing has fueled every war there ever was here, economics and greed is a big factor. Their basic instincts have never been managed."

"I'm aware of that General. Are they able to function without war? That's the question. Joshua, are you prepared for the "history lesson" you have to give?"

"Yes Sir, I have it broken down into a video format that even they could understand."

Captain Schultz, General Heinz and I then left the round table and went to the bridge together. I stood at the large window and looked down on Washington D.C. I looked at all the monuments and the architecture that adorned them, and realized it was borrowed from the Greeks and Romans years ago. I observed the grid layout of the streets of D.C. and saw how they formed a star from the galaxy they just left. It is a layout that can be seen from space, and was designed by one of our clones who lived here four hundred years ago. Our clones were also instrumental in designing their Constitution. He also noticed their belief in a God and how it began thousands of years ago, and how it still transcended into their daily lives. He stared for a minute and wondered if the Earthlings were indeed ready for peace, being that their DNA had been altered so many times.

"Solomon, are your aides preparing an answer for the Browns?"

"Yes, Isaac, I should have it within the hour. You do know we have the capability now to annihilate them?"

"I do. I'm also aware of the ramifications of this act. We are a peace-seeking people and will delay violence at all costs. They have always outnumbered us, but due to our leaps and bounds in dark matter, we have always been able to stay one step in front of them-- even though they now control and populate seventeen hundred planets. This time is different, though. We have fought them in the past, but never to the death. Extinguishing their whole armada will lead to an inter-galactic war, which we must avoid at all costs. Why can't they accept peace? Why does it always come to this? Is galactic dominance and stirring the pot that important to them?"

"Well, you know violence is still harbored in their DNA and they have resisted the need to change for eons. Isaac, I am also convinced that they are not aware of our new weapon, or they wouldn't be heading in this direction. In the past, they have always used acts of terrorism with subversive groups that were beamed down onto our planet and are doing the same here. Khartoum is a very competent leader and too smart to attack us if he knew we had a new weapon; therefore, I believe he doesn't know about it. My opinion is he'll have a show of force and wait until we leave to stir the pot once again."

"These are dangerous times, but no different than the differences we had in the past. It simply would be best if he backed off. If I threatened him with the weapon, he would take it as a sign of weakness and challenge me. Solomon, we may be forced to "demonstrate" it on one of his starships, thus killing all of its inhabitants."

"I'm afraid so. I hope he is rational. It is he who has enticed the fanaticism and terrorism that exists on Earth. I'm also sure he would like it to continue, because it's galaxy domination he's after."

"Why is it we're the peace makers in this Solar System, Solomon? It seems we go to one hot spot after another. What a stupid question. Forgive me. We all know the answer to that." I then looked at Adam. "Adam, this will be a profound and eventful meeting for the Earthlings. I want your crew to show the utmost hospitality while they're onboard. Will any of our robotic clones from Earth be attending the meeting?"

"Yes Sir. We have a nuclear scientist from M.I.T. and a Nuclear Physicist from Berkeley attending, as well as Computer Scientist from Stanford and Ohio State University. They have been on Earth for twenty-five to thirty-seven of their years. Each discipline is replaced every fifty years. We will scan each individual upon entering our ship so that there are no robotic moles from the Browns attending. If they do attempt entry, we are prepared to make them inoperable."

After Captain Schultz prepared his staff for the oncoming shuttles, he and the General and I returned to the round table.

"Captain, do we have communication with Commander Khartoum yet?"

"The transmission should be arriving within a couple of minutes, Sir, but we have been eavesdropping on him. It appears his mission is to stop us from disarming his allies in India, Iran and the States of Northern Africa."

"Alright, let's take our places."

As I waited for the transmission, I cupped my hands over my glass of water and stared at it. I then looked at one of the screens with a picture of Earth rotating on it and saw the blue planet covered with the large oceans of water. I knew that water was the life sustaining property that was needed for every life form with a large mental capacity, and it was these planets only that harbored civilized life. Water was the common denominator, as it is water that produces food and much needed oxygen for life.

"It's beautiful from above, Joshua. One would never know how congested it becomes once you descend."

CHAPTER ELEVEN
The Ultimatum

As I pondered the gift of life, Captain Schultz interrupted me. "Commander, we have Commander Khartoum on the wall."

I stared at the hologram of Khartoum and studied him before he spoke. Khartoum was a comparatively young man of one hundred and seven years, forty years older than me. He stood about seven feet tall and was on the heavy side. He had attended the Intergalactic School of Astronomical Sciences as well as Jupiter's War College. He has been a commander for thirty-three years and is solely responsible for creating the "Evil Axis" on Earth. His robotic clones have been assisting the powers in the Middle East in nuclear science and warfare for years. He was the key contributor to the violence when Iran attacked Israel in 2020 with nuclear weapons and was instrumental in helping India develop a satellite with laser capabilities. Khartoum was indeed a dangerous man, very intelligent, and void of human emotion. He was cold and calculating.

"Commander Glock, as we speak, I see you are occupying Earth. That is in direct conflict with our galactic laws and cause for immediate retribution. As you know, we are en route to intercept you, and I assume you are aware of that, and that is why you are trying to communicate with me."

Commander Khartoum was very aggressive by nature and achieved his position by not only outwitting his foes, but by sheer use of power and lack of fear. It's his style to have the numbers in his favor and today was no exception. He spoke with authority and feared no one.

"Commander Khartoum, we are here not to occupy, but to educate. It is no secret you are a war monger, and it is also no secret that we are a people of peace. We are here to disarm the Earthlings, as they have acquired nuclear-tipped satellites and missiles that can be used in space. We simply will not allow that. It is a violation of galactic law to use nuclear weapons in space and you are indeed aware of that. When we have completed our mission, we will leave."

"What makes you people think you are the advocates of peace? Although you preach peace, your weapons are highly developed, developed to the point of being devastating. I'm afraid we are going to have to oversee your activities while you're there. You see, we simply don't trust you. You have been supplying the Americans, Russians, Europeans and Israelis with superior weapons for years and this might just be another excuse to do so."

"Commander Khartoum, we do not need any interference from you. Just as you don't trust us, we don't trust you. You have a track record of harboring violence, and I advise you to turn around immediately or face the consequences."

"What consequences?" Khartoum asked. "We outnumber you 2-1. It is you that should be worried," as he laughed.

"Commander Khartoum, I am trying to have a meaningful dialogue with you, but you are being unreasonable. Yes, you do outnumber us 2-1, but what good is your advantage if you can't get off? We are in control of a new weapon that can annihilate you and your whole fleet. I ask you again to turn around or I will be forced to give you a demonstration."

I knew he had to fight fire with fire. Aggressiveness is the only thing Khartoum understands. I, more than anyone, knew the importance of achieving peace through strength, to be so strong that everyone feared you.

Commander Khartoum turned to his Lt. Commander and turned off the hologram while he spoke, "What is he talking about Abdul? Are you aware of a new weapon they may have?"

Abdul Hussein has been Commander Khartoum's assistant for six years now. He was versed in nuclear physics and Quantum Mechanics, as well as galactic warfare. He was very capable and next in line to the commander.

"Muhammad, there have been rumors of a new weapon, but no substantial proof. If they are in possession of a new weapon, there is no evidence of them ever using it."

"Captain Aseem, please scan their ships for nuclear plasma while we speak. It will be very dense, much denser than gold. We are searching for any indication of a new weapon system. Abdul, when will we enter Earth's atmosphere?"

Nassar Aseem was the captain of the Sphinx, the star ship Commander Khartoum used as a base. He was very competent, schooled in nuclear physics and galactic warfare too. He once led an ambush and destruction of 200 of the Yellows' fleet on the planet Tai Wai in the Andromeda Galaxy, thus garnering respect from Commander Khartoum.

"Yes Commander, it should take several minutes to scan their ships and get a response because of our distance to them."

While Captain Aseem scanned the mother ships on Earth, Abdul scanned the computer. "Commander, we could be there in eight days if we drop our sails. However, in doing so will cut into the energy level of our weapons."

Khartoum then stared at his monitor and asked Aseem to speed up the flight. "I understand, but we have to get there before Glock does irreparable damage to our allies."

When I saw the hologram go blank, he turned to Joshua. "Joshua, I think we sprung a nerve with them. My guess is they're scanning our ships for weapons before he makes a decision. Our nuclear plasma should be visible to their infrared detector. But just the presence of nuclear plasma won't dictate the extent of our weapon. He'll still be wondering what we may have, if anything."

"Yes Isaac, I fear his aggressive personality will push us to the limit. Hopefully, removing one of his star ships will sway him."

"Our mother ships should be in position on Mars in three and a half days, a day and a half before Khartoum gets there. We have four days to convince them to turn around."

While Joshua and I spoke, miles away at the entrance to our solar system, Commander Khartoum was deciphering the scanning of the mother ships. "There is a large presence of nuclear plasma evident on each ship, too much for ordinary weapons," Abdul said. "I fear they may be in control of a new weapon, the weapon that we have heard about."

"What could it be, Abdul? It can't be a new weapon. Surely each ship wouldn't have it. They have never demonstrated a new weapon on anybody. How much more powerful could weapons become? We have shields and we can be cloaked. How can they get to us?"

"At this time, I can't answer that. I do know they have been perfecting dark matter. What this entails, we could only guess; however, that is the worst-case scenario. I suggest we call their bluff. We do have them outnumbered."

"Okay. Captain Aseem, place Commander Glock on our screen."

As the hologram of Commander Glock appeared in the war room of Commander Khartoum, Commander Khartoum's aides sat assembled at the table. "Commander Glock, we have discussed your threat to us and we have decided to continue on our path. Our investment in the people of planet Earth is as great as yours. It would be imprudent and irresponsible to allow you to have your way here. I must remind you if you are planning an attack that we outnumber you almost 2-1. I will await your reply."

I then turned to Joshua, "Let's show them how selective and how destructively secretive we can be. Instead of taking out a star ship and creating a war, let's remove a sail from one of their ships, leaving it without their source of solar power."

"Commander, on which ship would you like to concentrate?"

"Joshua, aggression is the only thing Khartoum understands. Let's remove the sail from his ship. His ship is highly guarded, and he alone will feel our power. After his sail is gone, he could rely on nuclear power, or shuttle to another ship if necessary. This should get his attention. He'll then know how vulnerable he is."

"You do know that an extreme amount of dark energy will have to be expended to remove the sails. They are half a mile wide and made of dense gold foil. We may have to have two mother ships fire simultaneously to accomplish that, and we would diminish the defensive capabilities of those two ships tremendously."

"Yes, I know, Joshua, but it is important that they do this, and that they fire at the same time."

Joshua turned to Captain Shultz and gave the order to remove the sail immediately, and not wait until the mother ships reach Mars. Not wanting to give up the positions of the ships heading to Mars, Captain Shultz then contacted Captain Winters and Captain Schmidt on two of the ships that were hovering over Europe, and gave the order to ascend to 200 miles and fire. Because they could bend space with dark energy, the attack and destruction will be almost instantaneous. I then turned to Captain Schultz and told him to convey the message to the fleet of mother ships to continue their trip to Mars in case Commander Khartoum doesn't decide to turn his fleet around.

Meanwhile, Commander Khartoum was conferring with his military aides when his ship lost solar power and began to slow down. Although he had been traveling at 300,000 miles per hour, without the energy from solar photons, he was slowed down considerably. He simply was astonished at the loss of his sails without damage to his ship, and dumbfounded at the quick and instantaneous attack. He was simply blindsided by a sucker punch. He didn't see it coming and quickly realized his vulnerability.

He looked at his faithful assistant and spoke, "Abdul, I am in awe. We were cloaked, and millions of miles from them; yet they were not only able to attack us instantly. They were able to be selective in their target. It appears they could have done whatever they wanted. I do not want to negotiate in weakness; yet their new weapon renders us to be ineffective against them. Although we have a larger fleet, we cannot match their new weapon. I am at a loss for words."

"Commander, I suggest you have dialogue with Commander Glock and find out what his true intentions are. Do not show weakness, but instead show a concern for the galactic community in regards to the Earthlings' atomic weapons. We need time to regroup. We need to stall to enable us to get closer to them for our weapons to be effective. It is apparent they have controlled dark matter and dark energy, and in doing so, have bent space. It is even possible they may not let us get closer."

Meanwhile, back on Earth, as Assistant Commander Stonecypher and I were discussing the chess game Commander Khartoum might want to play, they were interrupted by Commander Khartoum on the hologram wall.

"Commander Glock, this is an act of war. I demand you cease your operations or pay the price. Do you really think you can harness enough energy to destroy my fleet? And if you are so fortunate to do so, you will be met with the full force of our people. I have already communicated your position to

Galactic Headquarters and the other armadas we control. They are readying a response."

I was seated at the round table when Commander Khartoum spoke. I then turned off the hologram, ceasing communication with Commander Khartoum, and turned to my aides and asked for their opinion on the matter.

"Commander, it is bravado to which he speaks," said Assistant Commander Joshua Stonecypher. "Because of our history of never initiating combat, he doesn't really expect you to commit to an act of war. I suggest we disable the two star ships to each side of him, and threaten him with the annihilation of his ship if he doesn't comply. After all, it is war he wants and we are just protecting ourselves."

I absorbed the recommendation and then looked at General Heinz, "Solomon, are we physically prepared for an all-out skirmish with the Browns? Can we control enough dark matter to attack them from this distance and still have enough energy to return home?"

"Commander, we can technically destroy them, but in doing so will leave us without enough energy to navigate home through worm holes. Their star ships are huge and numerous, and destroying them requires a lot of energy. We essentially would be lost in space until we could replenish our dark energy. We would have to find a planet with the elements necessary to create more exotic matter, and none exists in this Solar System except Earth. We would have to mine in plain view of the Earthlings."

"Solomon, we have a couple of problems here. Because of our precarious situation and our location over Earth, we would have to have a minimum amount of collateral damage and we would have to keep this engagement with the Browns from the Earthlings. After all, we are here on a mission of peace and education. A war in space would lower our credibility with them."

"Commander, I'm aware of that. That's why you had our two ships climb to 200 miles before firing. Because of our new weapon system, we can keep collateral damage to a minimum. As far as the Earthlings are concerned, they won't even know about our skirmish because their satellites and observatories are shut off. We have until our fleet reaches the back side of Mars to decide what you'd like to do. We have less than four days to decide our course of action. Of course, if you dismantle more sails, it would buy us even more time. They would be slowed down considerably and the energy lost from their sails would preclude them from waging a full-fledged war."

"Thank you, Solomon. I like Joshua's recommendation. Are you in agreement with this strategy?"

"I am Commander. Removing two more sails from his flanks should wake him up and perhaps turn him around. However, that will leave us with six ships with depleted power plants."

"Adam, give the command to Captain Winters to remove the sails from the two ships that flank him and notify the others to continue their course to Mars."

"Yes Sir. It is done."

"Thank you. Adam, please keep me informed of their status. We have three days to decide what to do with the Browns if they don't comply. Feel free to consult Joshua if you need him for anything that may arise."

Four hours later, as I continued to speak to my aides, the wall lit up with a hologram of Commander Khartoum speaking.

"Commander Glock, you are clearly in possession of a secret weapon and are in violation of galactic law. What you have done to my three star ships is now an act of war."

"Commander Khartoum, we are a peaceful people and try to maintain peace in the galaxy. You are a war-faring people and would only complicate our mission, which is to disarm the Earthlings use of nuclear weapons in space. That is a violation and in direct disharmony with galactic law. They will be stopped with or without your interference. What we have done to you is minor to what we could have done. The choice is yours. If you don't turn around, you will be met with a force that will be swift and deadly, and I will be in full compliance with galactic law by eliminating your threat to peace. I will give you one hour to confer with your aides."

I then turned off the hologram and walked to the large window in the room that faced Washington D.C. below me. With my back to the round table, I spoke, "It has been thousands of years since we had a confrontation with the Browns over the planet Earth. We repelled them then, and it looks like we may have to do it again. The only thing that separates our weapon development from them is our great advances in quantum mechanics and quantum gravity. We must never let them capture a mother ship. They would spend no time reverse engineering our accomplishments. We would then have hell to pay."

As I contemplated their next move, Adam interrupted me, "Commander, we will be accepting our first shuttle within the hour, and the remainder of them should arrive within two hours."

"Thank you, Adam. Have your welcoming committee prepare for their arrival. Make sure they accidentally catch a glimpse of our saucers and observatory while they walk to the assembly hall. It is important they are impressed."

Chapter Twelve
Glitches

As nightfall swept over Washington D.C., the residents looked skyward as the large metallic mother ship, glowing in the sky, illuminated the city with an eerie aura. There was no noise coming from it, just the pale-yellow glow with the outer portion of the hub spinning slowly, like a giant cartwheel. Air traffic and all means of transportation had been shut off by the aliens, essentially cutting off the electrical impulse that all vehicles need to operate. People were anxious and confused, and watched their holograms at home for any news that may be leaked. The aliens would let the communication satellites operate only when they wanted to communicate with the people, so there was no pre-described timetable or time limit. People had to simply watch and wait and hope for the best. They already knew that the best scientists and engineers in the world were being gathered for an historic meeting and that the aliens were here for a peaceful mission--at least that's what they were told. There were as many people standing in the streets looking upward as there were staring at their blank hologram wall in their house, waiting for it to be activated. Everyone wanted information, information of any kind. While the common man was watching the walls of his house for the latest hologram, the politicians of Washington were whisked away to concrete bunkers under the Capital Building and White House. These bunkers were connected by a tunnel which housed a high-speed rail that went all the way to a secret installation in Colorado.

The larger than life monuments of the city glowed with a faint incandescent glow. The Washington Monument, the Jefferson Memorial, and the Lincoln Memorial all appeared to be looking skyward. The Korean Memorial with the large bronze soldiers walking up the hillside in the fog with their guns in hand appeared more meaningful than ever. The yellow color that emanated onto them from above appeared as they were indeed involved in a wartime situation, as if they were walking into hell. The flat, black granite wall of the Vietnam Memorial looked like a giant mirror glowing in the night, and the water in the Washington Mall reflected the mother ship above. The new Kennedy Memorial, built in 2063 and overlooking the eternal flame in Arlington, was also aglow with yellow light. Fear gripped the city.

High above the capital, the center of the hub of the ship quietly opened its doors and awaited their first arrival. The shuttles were cigar-shaped and were nuclear powered, being approximately eighty feet long and twenty feet wide by twenty feet tall. They were supersonic, and could travel at Mach 12 in Earth's atmosphere. In other words, from Europe to Washington D.C. in thirty minutes, on an arc that momentarily took them into the fringe of space. Assistant Commander Steinbrenner and I stood in the Bridge and oversaw the arrival of shuttles from all over the globe. They each carried the best scientists from all over the world, each a specialist in his own discipline. Today would be momentous for Earthlings and the information they received today would not only alter their most basic instincts, but change their concept of time, religion, and science. I knew that this would be traumatic to them and would have to be initiated very carefully to be meaningful.

The shuttle that carried scientists from the United States arrived first and carried mathematicians, nuclear scientists, chemistry professors, physic, and biology scientists, as well as a consortium of anthropologists and archeologists, twenty-five in all. They were the best America had to offer, and represented the best universities, corporations and think tanks in the country. As they sat in the shuttle, they discussed the magnitude of this trip and were already in awe of the nuclear shuttle that transported them and the speed it attained. It also carried engineers from Amazon, Boeing, Northrup, Rocketdyne and Samsung, who studied the details of the shuttle closely as they conversed. As they looked out the window, even though it was night, they could see the vastness of the ship's size as they approached it and other shuttles stacking up in a landing path behind them. The opening to the mother ship was huge, and as they approached the opening for a landing, the giant shadow that the mother ship cast obliterated any light there might have been momentarily.

Upon entering the mother ship, they saw a large name on the side of the ship--"Vesuvius" is what it said. The terminal was large and well-lit, not with lights but with walls that were illuminated with a glow that was soothing to the eyes. They saw people walking around the perimeter of the metallic tarmac, and were relieved somewhat that they looked human. They were built in the same image as the Earthlings, but taller. Each one appeared to be at least seven feet tall. They were all dressed in white uniforms and boots, and wore no masks. It appeared that breathing oxygen wasn't a problem for them. Their body structure and gait was similar to the Earthlings, except for their skull, which appeared to be large and elongated. They didn't know they were looking at androids. The shuttle didn't glide in for its landing, but levitated above its landing designation and slowly descended, all without any noise from its source of power. It was all very smooth and impressive, especially to the engineers.

Captain Shultz and his aides waited on the tarmac for the shuttle to open its doors, waiting for the first visitors from Earth. As the door to the shuttle opened, a metallic ramp extended from the ship to the tarmac and the scientists and engineers deplaned. They were cordially met by Captain Schultz. "Gentlemen, welcome to the Vesuvius. I am Captain Adam Schultz. This is indeed a momentous event for both of us. You are the first of your generation to experience a meeting with aliens from another planet. Your vital signs are being recorded as we speak, and I see you have much apprehension. I assure you that you have nothing to fear. We are here in peace and you will leave here with a new understanding of your place in the cosmos. We have demanded you board without any image-capturing devices and electrical or communicating devices for a reason. Hologram recording devices will be issued to each of you in which you can take with you and download when you return to Earth. My aides will escort you to the assembly hall where we will await the arrival of other scientists and 35 engineers from the globe. You are our guests here, and if there is something you want, feel free to ask. We have food and drink that each nationality desires."

As they walked the large perimeter of the space port on the way to the assembly hall, a hangar door was left partially open, leaving the scientists to observe a fleet of one hundred saucer-shaped vehicles levitating two feet above the tarmac floor, all blinking with a faint glow of light with no noise being emitted. They looked at each other in silence and amazement without talking. My ploy seemed to be working. They were in awe. While they walked, they looked upward to the large glass ceiling that covered the hangar and tarmac, and saw the largest telescope they had ever seen. It dwarfed the Hummel III telescope that was sent into space years earlier, and simply amazed the Earthlings.

Meanwhile, on the bridge, I was summoned to the round table. Commander Khartoum was waiting on their hologram again. I gathered Joshua and took the transporter to the round table where General Heinz and his aides were waiting. I sat at the table, pushed a button, and Commander Khartoum was on the screen.

"Commander Glock, I have conferred with President Chong of the Federated Galactic Council and relayed our situation to him with your proposed intentions. Although you are right in disarming nuclear warheads from being used in space, you are wrong in attacking our ships without provocation. I'm quite sure he has been in contact with you. We are coming to Earth to observe and ensure you don't try to overturn the balance of power in your favor. The American, Russian and European armies already hold an advantage over our allies in India and Africa, and we won't allow any more knowledge of weapons released to them. Your actions are being reported to the Council, and sanctions will be placed upon you when you return."

I turned off the hologram and looked at Solomon. "Solomon, they can be here in eight days or less, and I don't believe they are coming here to observe. I believe in clear conscience that we are in the right by disabling the remainder of their ships."

"Yes Isaac, I concur with you. The Council knows their modus operandi and knows they have never sought peace. By removing the sails from their remaining ships, it will lengthen their ETA by another eight days, and leave them floundering in space. That is the "Achilles heel" of their propulsion system. We should be done with our mission here by then. The question will then arise, what do we do with them when we're done on Earth? We can't leave them here to exploit the planet. That is exactly what they'll do when they're disabled--once the nuclear-tipped missiles are disarmed and we depart."

"Joshua, what are your feelings on this?"

"Isaac, it is evident we have to slow them down. Khartoum is too predictable. We know all he wants is to get closer to us, to get us in his sights. He still thinks his advantage in numbers is enough when he is close enough. He did the same thing when he annihilated Commander Lee of the Yellow Army fifty years ago in Sirius. Although Lee had a tactical advantage, Khartoum outnumbered his forces as they do ours now. Our advantage is the control of dark energy, which allows us to attack from great distances. We must not lose our advantage."

"Okay, removing their sails slows them down. I feel after disabling them, it will still lead to war, and we will be forced to erase them. Then we will have the Galactic Council to deal with."

"Isaac, what sanctions can they place on us, and how can they enforce the sanctions? Our planet is economically feasible, relying on no one, and our mother ships are second to none. If there's a mineral we need, we know where to go to mine it. We are economically and energy untouchable."

"Yes Joshua, but throughout our history, we have never been the aggressor. We are known for defending the downtrodden, and now we are faced with annihilating an entire army. Let it be recorded, Khartoum was warned to back off and still advanced on us."

I then turned the hologram back on and faced Khartoum. "Commander, you leave us no choice. I repeat my demand. You must turn around now or face the consequences."

"Commander Glock, apparently you don't know the law of the cosmos. It is you that are wrong for attacking us."

I then turned off the hologram and reluctantly gave the order to Captain Schultz to disable and remove the sails from the remaining armada. Captain Schultz then called the fleet that Captain Winters controlled and gave the order. Captain Winters then called back to confirm the order. Within minutes, Commander Khartoum's entire armada was disabled, slowing their speed in half and making them rely on their nuclear capabilities for power. Khartoum was furious and summoned his best nuclear engineer to his side. "Amman, do we have enough energy to go to war with the Whites? And if we do, do we have enough energy to make it home afterwards?"

"Commander, we rely on the sails for most of our power and now they are gone. We cannot wage a war and have the energy to make it back to our planet. We cannot do both. We would have to stop and mine the uranium and plutonium we need to refuel. Otherwise, we will die in space."

"Aseem, get us to the backside of their Moon. Perhaps we can ambush them on their return from Earth. An ambush of close proximity is our only chance of retaliation at this point. It would take too long for reinforcements to arrive here to help us. Cloak our ships so our presence is not known. Get me Commander Glock on the wall again."

"Commander, you forget our cloak is not an option anymore. They eliminated our sails while we were cloaked; therefore, they will know we are heading their way."

"Aseem, you are correct. Get me Commander Hussein at Pyramid Control. We will need reinforcements. Relay the extent of their new weapon and have our research department try to develop an answer for it." Khartoum then pushed the hologram button. "Commander Glock, you leave us no choice but to turn around and live to fight another day. I can assure you that you have not had the last word in this matter."

I stared at the screen and then turned to my reliable aide Joshua. "Joshua, it appears we have bought some time, but I know him. Relay our status to Captain Maro. Have him continue his flight to Mars, and tell him to be on the lookout for anything unusual. I am quite sure we have not heard the last of Khartoum."

Chapter Thirteen
History 101

As the events transpired in the war room, I was summoned from the round table to the bridge, as the last of the shuttles had arrived from Europe and the Middle East. When I arrived there, I was met by General Gunter of the Special Security Service.

"Commander, we have seven clones in custody from the Brown contingent from Iran, Pakistan, and India, who tried to board the ship. They are being held in the lower chamber. Their computer devices have been deactivated, and we have downloaded their memory. It appears they were going to try to sabotage our ship for Commander Khartoum. They were equipped with a homing device that was to seek out our dark energy chamber. We disabled them in their shuttles while en route to Washington by jamming their circuits. The Earthlings didn't know they were clones, and thought there was a medical problem because they slumped over in their seat. They have no idea what happened."

"Thank you, General Gunter. It was handled very professionally. Contact General Heinz and notify him of your finding and subsequent action. I'm sure Khartoum will be interested too."

While we spoke, a European shuttle arrived and deplaned. It was then I cast my eyes upon her for the first time. A petite Bio-Nuclear scientist from Italy stepped off her transport and locked eyes with me, stopping me in my tracks. I had been in space for two years this deployment, without sexual gratification of any kind and I thought I was looking at a dream, at poetry in motion. She was two feet shorter than me and my mind entertained the possibilities that could take place. I knew the rules--no sexual contact with Earthlings because of their violent DNA genes and the deadly virus' they carry, but I was mesmerized by her beauty. Her black olive eyes and bronze body were a striking contrast to my blue eyes and pale skin. Sensing my interest in her, she coyly tugged at the bun her black hair was in and smiled at me, exposing a dimple in her cheek. Her white smock hid her attributes, but her legs were tanned and well-shaped in the heels she wore. Although she was with a host of other scientists, I looked at her name tag and made an excuse to talk to her.

"Miss Aiello, I am Commander Glock. Welcome to Vesuvius. I see you are versed in Nuclear Biology. How long have you been in this field?"

"Hello Commander," smiling while she talked. "I have been a scientist for 15 years now, with Nuclear DNA my specialty. I am in awe of your ship, Commander. What an honor it would be to see more of it."

"Perhaps after your briefing, I can arrange that Miss Aiello," as I smiled and noticeably glanced at her figure. "But first maybe you should move along. It will be starting soon. Thank you for your interest."

While Commander Glock spoke, Dr. Gilmore scanned the hologram screen and checked Glock's vitals and brain waves. She then watched Glock speak and wanted to interrupt, but decided to wait until he was done. It was evident that Miss Aiello left an impression on him.

Glock continued, "I couldn't help but look at her as she smiled and walked away. She then joined her group and was transported to the assembly hall with the others. I then gathered Assistant Commander Steinbrenner and General Heinz, and took the transporter to the assembly hall where the world was filing in and waiting. The assembly hall was huge, designed with stadium seating, and had a occupancy of 1500 people that was used for training and informational feeds as necessary. Today the seats were filled to capacity. Being the aliens were all over seven feet tall, the seats were a little uncomfortable for the Earthlings. Most of them sat with their feet dangling in the air. The walls were illuminated softly as it was in the hangar. Each seat had its own hologram screen, as well as a huge hologram screen on the stage behind the podium. The Earthlings sat while a hushed buzz of discussion among them filled the air. As the three representatives of the Vesuvius entered the hall, the scientists and engineers of planet Earth stood in respect. There was no applause, just a silent and cautious respect as they waited in apprehension.

I then took the podium, "Ladies and Gentleman, I am Commander Isaac Glock. This is General Solomon Heinz and this is my Assistant Commander Joshua Steinbrenner.

Joshua will be conducting this interview with you today and has developed an interesting and chronological time period for not only your planet, but the universe as well. As you can see, there are no politicians present for the following reasons. What we are discussing today is of scientific value, and we feel politicians have their own priorities at hand and not the values of the people. Additionally, and quite frankly, I don't think they would fully comprehend the complexity of our representation. As you know, we are here to educate you in the use of nuclear power and to tell you that nuclear weapons will not be used in space, not now, not ever. There are many things about science and nuclear physics that you cannot comprehend at this time. You are on page five of a large novel. We are prepared to disarm you of any and all nuclear capabilities if these principles are not understood. You are representatives of your solar system now and must abide by the rules. We can also educate you in the safe use of nuclear energy, and perhaps enlighten you on how better to feed your planet and derive the best use of energy possible. Basically, you are a war mongering people and this aggression must stop. I don't want to open the floor for discussion at this time. I prefer you to watch your screens and absorb the information first. Hopefully, your questions will be answered as we continue. You have stared at the heavens for eons, and for eons you thought you were special, that all this was created just for you. What you learn today will disband those theories. I will now turn this over to Joshua, who will narrate this dissertation."

Assistant Commander Joshua Stonecypher took the podium and introduced himself. He was over seven feet tall and very imposing, being well versed in universal history and the nuclear sciences. As he began to speak, the hologram wall and the screens at each seat lit up simultaneously. He walked over to the screen and touched it. "In the beginning, your scientists refer to the "Big Bang" as the beginning and catalyst for the Universe approximately 14 billion years ago. You are partly right. In fact, there wasn't a "Big Bang" at all, but instead a "Big Bounce." Your scientists discovered the entity known as the "Black Hole," which is a vortex that increases gravitational pull and sucks up everything in its sight or neighborhood. As this matter is funneled to the center of the black hole, mass becomes so dense that it collapses upon itself. As it goes, there was a universe before ours, and perhaps one before that. It is a cycle that keeps repeating itself like the seasons on Earth. The universe collapses upon itself through the ever-growing black hole until it can no longer control the energy it has consumed, and then blows and starts expanding again, thus the big bounce. Gravity started the collapse and to understand this, you must understand Quantum Gravity. This takes over where the Theory of Relativity ends. This universe had an ancestor born inside a black hole. The theory that matter doesn't disappear but instead changes shape is true. This theory is all mathematical and we can prove it to you.

For years you have been stalled on the Theory of Relativity, a theory that our clones had given you. Yes, we have had clones on your planet bringing you along gradually in the sciences for years, and some of them are seated with you tonight." They stopped looking at the screen and looked at each other, wondering who was a clone? Joshua continued, "General Relativity is not the complete theory. It is the beginning and it is shouting at you, telling you there is so much more. It is "A" on the way to "Z". For a universe to prosper, it must reproduce and create black holes that collapse, become denser, and then explode again. As there is a cycle of life and death on this planet, so is there one in space. If the Universe didn't reinvent itself, it would simply die. The Big Bang didn't come from nothing, but from something, essentially the former universe that collapsed. I know it is a puzzling paradox. Nothing is something. Every action has an opposite and equal reaction. It is a cycle that keeps repeating itself. What you call empty space, or a vacuum, is actually dark energy. It's all mathematical and like I said, we will prove it to you before we leave. You must study the theory of Quantum Mechanics to study the void you call space, and Quantum Gravity to become more knowledgeable in black holes."

As Joshua spoke, the scientists saw black holes formed and up close for the first time on their screens. They saw stars and solar systems sucked through their vortex, which was so much more than the Carl Sagan Telescope had given them. It was an awe-inspiring trip through space that had only been imagined before.

Joshua continued, "The universe is so much larger than you can imagine, and is divided into four quadrants. We have already explained to you why it is expanding. The universe is approximately 14 billion years old, our Solar System is 6 billion years old and yours is 4.5 billion years old. Here is our star system in the Orion belt. Our planet is called Hercules and is twice as large as Earth. It revolves around a binary star system, and yes, as you can see, we have two Suns. Our climate is similar to yours as well as the chemical makeup and gravity index. There are 50 billion planets in the universe with approximately 1% of them that sustain life as we know it. That's 500,000,000 planets with human life, with the presence of water and oxygen being the common denominator."

A scientist from Germany then raised his hand, as if to want to ask a question. Joshua turned to him and said, "There will be no question and answer period until the presentation is concluded. There is much for you to digest here, and each of you will be taking a copy of this seminar with you back to your prospective country. It will open new avenues of thinking and a different approach to your past and future."

Joshua continued speaking as the hologram lit up again. "You know how, and you know how long ago your planet was formed, so we don't have to cover that. We are here to educate you on what you don't know and to enlighten you on your past history. Your Earth is one of many ideal planets in this universe that sustains life. You have skin instead of fur because of your climate. Some of the animals on your planet can be found on other planets as the prime species there. They simply had to adapt to their respective climates as you have adjusted here. The ecology of the planet, as well as the density of the atmosphere, including gravity, will determine the makeup of the specie."

Joshua stopped the hologram and looked directly at the seated crowd. "What is next may be very surprising to you and may be startling. We have video of our ancestors' first visit here 400,000 years ago. We first sent probes here as you are doing now in your solar system. We then came to mine the planet for precious minerals and were exposed to your ancestors, who were nothing more than erect apes at the time. We were not the only visitors to this planet. You have been visited by many others, and many have exploited your planet for its wealth of raw materials. We are called the Whites, but you have been visited and inhabited not only by us, but by the Browns, the Blacks, the Yellows, the Grays, and the Reptilians. Only the Grays and the Reptilians found your planet too inhospitable to sustain their life. As you look around the room, it is no coincidence that your race and language coincides with past visitors to this planet. When we first visited here years ago, the brain mass of your ancestors was very small and their intelligence was very limited. At first, we interbred with them artificially to genetically speed up their development and to increase their brain mass. Our motives were selfish, as we used them for slaves to do our mining. You were a violent species, and as time went by, we and other aliens started dumping our criminals and lowlifes here, essentially interbreeding amongst them. We studied them and periodically enhanced their biological makeup, advancing their civilization gradually. Violence has been removed from our DNA thousands of years ago, but is still harbored in other aliens. We have tried to remove the violence gene from your biological makeup, but due to the many catastrophic events that happen here and because of the visits from other aliens and your migrations on the planet, it has been impossible. Before I continue, we should take a break."

Joshua turned off the hologram and screens and illuminated the huge room. Robotic androids of the Whites served refreshments, all the while, undetected by the scientists. The room was alive with discussions carried on in every corner. Everyone had a thousand questions. While they talked, Joshua left the room and transported himself to the bridge where he met up with me. "Joshua, I've been watching your presentation and the amazement of the Earthlings. We have been recording their vital signs and they are quite excited. Do you think they can handle the meat of the presentation? Are they ready to grow up?"

"I don't know, Sir. They appear to have many questions, but what has to be done, has to be done. I came to the bridge for the latest information regarding Khartoum. Has he turned around or is he still attempting to reach us?"

"According to our electromagnetic radiation screen and our eavesdropping, they are cloaked and are heading to the back side of the Moon to mine for the fuel they'll need to fight us and return to their planet. Khartoum is convinced that he could be victorious if he gets closer to us. Captain Phillips has been notified of our desire to stop them, as he has been monitoring them also. He will be on Mars a full three days before Khartoum passes. That will give him plenty of time to mine the exotic matter he needs to replenish the nuclear plasma that dark energy requires to man the weapons and defeat Khartoum. It took a lot of energy to remove the gold foil from his armada. If all goes well, they will be able to restore the dark energy while Khartoum is still miles away, allowing him to hit Khartoum in an ambush. He won't know what hit him."

Chapter Fourteen
The Gods

Joshua returned to the assembly hall and called the session to order. Before he could begin, an engineer from a think tank in America asked if it was possible to have a tour of the ship when the session was completed. Joshua looked at him and said, "I have been expecting that question. There will be a tour of the ship before you leave. Because of the amount of people involved, it won't be possible to give you a complete tour. Depending on your profession, some of you will be more interested in some things than others and because of that, we will try to make the tour as well-rounded as possible."

Joshua then turned from the podium and walked to the wall. Pensively, he looked at the floor before he spoke. "What I am divulging to you today essentially is eons of historical facts that your planet has hypothesized since the beginning of time. I know that some of you will doubt what I say, but you once thought that your world was flat too. It is a lot to comprehend in such a short time, but together with this dissertation and the microchip that you will be bringing with you back to your planet, you will have time to decipher this material and give it the credence it deserves."

Joshua then turned on the hologram again and began narrating, "You were born by natural selection but through the years, your genes have been altered many times by us and others. Hundreds of thousands of years ago your forefathers made a sudden giant leap in culture. For years, you have been looking for the "missing link," the bridge that brought you from caveman status to toolmakers. I'm here to tell you today that WE are the "missing link." It is our artificial interbreeding with your ancestors that suddenly increased your brain size and capacity for growth, thus jump starting your progress. That is why you haven't found the archeological ancestor that filled the gap between gatherer and tool maker. WE had made that sudden change in your development. When you fully learn to read the genetic code, you will see the intervention of our gene."

Joshua continued, "Not only have we had an influence on your culture, but the Browns, Blacks, and Yellows have also. Yes, there are others who have been here and they have settled in parts of the globe that closely resemble their home planet. When we mined gold and uranium here eons ago, the natives referred to us as the Anunnakis.

You believe that all life on your planet emanated from Africa. Do you really believe that the color of your skin changes depending on your location? That particular latitude circles the globe, and yet there is no other people on Earth with the characteristics found there. The yellows settled in now what you call India and Asia and had great influence there. The Blacks settled in Africa and were the first to settle on this planet. Because of your many migrations, interbreeding has taken place and some cultures were wiped out while some expanded and made new ethnicities. Your core language has remained, but colloquialisms have developed, thus creating the many languages you experience today. Because of the many catastrophic events on your planet, your planet has suffered amnesia. The advanced civilization you are now experiencing is not the first on your planet. There have been many others and they have been destroyed by your 26,000-year cycle of massive change, as well as galactic events that you cannot prepare for, such as severe quakes and strikes by asteroids.

Today is a historical event for you Earthlings and it could be extremely sensitive, because you have denied alien existence for years. You believe in a God, and actually believe that you are the only intelligent beings in the universe. This belief was inherent to your race by how we presented ourselves to you thousands of years ago. You see, because of our supernatural powers and your hindered brain development, your ancestors actually started believing in a God after our first visit. They thought we were gods and angels. Our backpacks, for navigating Earth were misconstrued for "wings" and were drawn and painted as "Angels". They simply figured if a man was flying, he had to have wings like a bird. Due to their misunderstanding and lack of technology, they recorded our events as God-like. You are right though. There is indeed a creator, but it is not us. He has visited your planet as He has visited ours. It is up to you to believe and change.

The last time we tried to jump start your planet was on an island off the European coast in the Mediterranean Sea. It was called Atlantis, and it was very advanced. We created a base there with a grid system that was identical to our mother ship, with an observatory in the center. We taught the Earthlings science and mathematics, and had heliports which we used as a base for exploring and mining the planet. We were there for about 5,000 years and during this time, your planet was going through the cycle where your poles melted and the sea waters rose. It is a natural occurrence, and is what you have been calling Global Warming. Because of the melting of the poles, the water was encroaching on the perimeter of our base when we were struck by a severe earthquake. The quake ultimately sunk the island and an underground volcano killed and covered all of its inhabitants, ultimately destroying our labs and all the good we had done. While we were there, we had actually removed the violent gene from the DNA of its citizens, but the scientific progress we had done was destroyed. The remainder of the Earth's inhabitants remained violent, and is violent to this day. The folklore of Atlantis was handed down to the Greeks and the Romans by scientists who were taught our principles outside of Atlantis, and I'm here to tell you today that Atlantis did exist and we can show you where it was located. Perhaps one day an archeologist will unearth a relic from the past. I will tell you this, Atlantis will be found under lava that has been solidified.

The room buzzed with excitement as they viewed Atlantis on the screen. They saw an advanced civilization with solar powered buildings and levitated vehicles, with communication systems that aren't even in existence today. There was actual footage of the quake and volcanic blast occurring, and the ensuing flood that destroyed the Island. Then much later, they saw other members of their fleet recovering scientific gear and the cameras that scanned the underwater city during the deluge. They saw saucers explore other areas of the planet at the time and enter the oceans at will, with no change in their velocity. They saw underwater bases and the oceans great rifts being mined for minerals.

They were in awe as they sat and watched in amazement.

"We were not the only aliens to influence your planet. The Browns established a civilization in an area you call Egypt about seven thousand of your years ago. They experimented with your DNA and created hybrids with human bodies. They created creatures with the body of a human and a head of an eagle, and the body of a lion with the head of a human. None of these were successfully bred and the specie soon died. Because of their advanced use of electromagnetism, they were able to defy the law of gravity and built large monuments, of which the layout of the Pyramids of Egypt assimilate the stars of Orion, their home and origin. The Great Temple of Karnak was built with huge stones in a pattern that is only visible from space. Their gods, Osiris and Isis, who was the symbol of life, was the most important deity Egypt ever had. They originally came from the star Sirius, which is about 8.5 light years from here, or six trillion miles to you, and since have migrated to the belt of Orion. They are a war mongering race and occupy many planets in the Universe. Their main goal is to occupy Earth, but as of this date we have repelled them, mainly because some of our ancestors also occupy Earth. Again, we remain a non-violent race, as the violent gene has been removed from our DNA."

Joshua continued, "We have occupied and jump started your genes through procreation over many eons. Your forefathers built monuments to honor us all around the globe. In Machu Picchu, our latest and most recent attempt at changing your culture, we set up a base around 1400 AD in the Andes Mountains of Peru. It was rich in minerals and we mined the area for gold, silver, and platinum. The Incas were a small people and indigenous to that area. We helped them build Machu Picchu atop a mountain, and gave them construction skills that weren't found anywhere else in the Americas. It had a natural spring which we gave a two-percent grade, and it flowed through the whole area, giving all fresh water for farming and sustaining the population. As you could see, the massive stones are cut with a laser and put in place by defying your laws of gravity. They are actually levitated by reversing electromagnetism. Your history books say that the city was built by them, which is impossible, as the stones are precision cut and fit into place so precisely that mortar wasn't needed. This would have taken them hundreds of years to accomplish without our intervention, if accomplished at all. Furthermore, because of an outbreak of smallpox, their civilization only lasted one hundred years, not nearly enough time to build anything this complex. Your scientists will find in the future that ALL viruses are caused by microbes deposited on this planet from space and microbes from dead bodies transmitted through the atmosphere. This includes microbes from decaying dead bodies and the dust they turn into.

On the Nazca Plains in Peru, as you can see, we actually scraped off the top of the mountains and deposited the soil miles away from the mountain. There was an abundance of gold and other rare minerals found in the area, and the port was used as a shuttling platform for our cigar shaped transports. The area was huge and could only be seen from space. We used the natives as slaves and taught them some of our ways. You can see the story they told of us on hieroglyphs, which are still visible on some of their caves.

On Easter Island, they erected giant statues 1,500 years ago to honor us, who they deemed as gods. The statues are giants, because they referred to us as giants. The natives stood barely five feet tall, whereas we stood over seven feet tall. As you can see on the screen, the large rocks that the statues were composed of came from miles away and were brought to their site by us. And, as you can see, the rocks are actually being levitated to their sites, defying gravity, and put in place. There was no way the natives of Easter Island could have done this by themselves.

In England, Stonehenge was erected about 5,000 years ago as a way of teaching astronomical events to the natives who dwelled there. Again, you can see the large stones being levitated and brought to the site.

In the Americas, the Mayans were the most intelligent group we encountered, as they learned our ways quickly. We taught them the periods of astronomical procession, and they were able to study the cosmos and devise a timely calendar of the heaven's movement.

You have discovered some of our ancestors and you will discover more. The skeletal remains of red-headed giants discovered in a cave in the Nevada desert, near Lovelock, Nevada, were two of our astronauts who got stranded here. Your mythical story of David and Goliath was true, only it isn't myth. Goliath was one of ours. He was a descendant of one of many criminals left behind when we mined Earth and used Earth as a dumping ground for fugitives.

Speaking of myths, when we occupied your oceans 100,000 years ago, we crossbred the top half of a human being with the dorsal fin of a dolphin. We needed help at the bottom of the ocean to mine the precious minerals needed for space travel. What we got was a humanoid with the intelligence and dexterity of a human being with a dorsal fin and webbed hands. You called them mermaids. Yes, there are mermaids and we created them. They have the same genetic DNA markers and similar traits as you humans. They lived and multiplied in the oceans for thousands of years and still do. As they adapted to the ocean, they developed sonar waves for communicating and hunting, much like the dolphins and whales they travel with. They are the source for your folklore, and perhaps someday you will find a skeleton or fossil of one. They were documented and seen by ancient Chinese, Greeks, Romans, and most recently by criminals you call pirates. Although your Navies have denied their existence, they are aware of them. They were also seen and documented by two of your great explorers, Christopher Columbus and Henry Hudson. Today, they travel and migrate with dolphins and whales, and use whales as a protection against orcas and sharks.

And Sasquatch? Yes, we created them about 1900 of your years ago. It was an experiment where we biologically created a life form by combining a gorilla with a human being to carry gold ore from mines. The specie had a hard time surviving because of its small brain mass.

Let's go back to fairly recent times. The Greeks called our past leaders gods and built large monuments to honor them too. The Acropolis, Delphi, the Parthenon, and the Temple of Apollo were all built to honor our forefathers. Zeus, one of our past stellar officers, was very powerful and a military man. The Greeks called him a "War God," while his brother Poseidon was called the "God of the Sea," as he would enter the sea frequently to visit the underwater base which was established in the Mediterranean. Apollo was a scientist who flew over the area often, and was a teacher to the scientists of the Greeks. The three were very powerful men and influenced their culture in many ways. A little later, the Romans called Zeus by the name of Jupiter, Poseidon's son was called Neptune, and Apollo's named remained Apollo. We influenced both the Greek and Roman cultures and being Zeus was a military officer, the Greeks and Romans were warfaring countries that ruled the ancient world for years. The Browns influenced the area you call the Middle East and Egyptian culture, while the Yellows influenced and interbred with the peoples of Asia and India. The races and languages became mixed, as people crossed the land bridges from one continent to another and learned to navigate the seas.

CHAPTER FIFTEEN
The Encounter

Joshua shut off the hologram and addressed the group. "I'm sure this video has destroyed your psyche. We have discussed the origin of many of your past myths and beliefs, and I am sure you have questions about a major belief that you harbor to this day. I have told you that Moses was a descendant of ours, which probably brought up more questions than answers. Before I continue, let's take a break. I'm sure you will converse and hypothesize about the big event in which your planet believes and shares, though it is told differently by most cultures. I am going to the bridge and will return in two hours. You are free to visit the dining room or wonder about the ship, but whatever you decide, please return in two hours. Thank you."

Before the scientists split up into groups and toured the ship, I messaged Scientist Aiello on her hologram to tell her an android would escort her to my table in the officers' dining room. Joshua then explained there was an area for each discipline to view, each being a treasure trove for scientists. As they toured the ship, Joshua returned to the bridge to meet with his staff, and I went to the Dining Room.

I had just sat down when she walked in, turning heads everywhere. I felt the palpitations in my chest as she glided across the floor, as if walking on air. I was smitten. I stood as she walked up to me, looking down on her with our eyes meeting in a big smile. I enveloped her tiny hand as I shook it, noticing the perspiration on her palms. And although it was just a handshake, I didn't want to let go."

At this point all six members turned their head to Commander Glock and the Hologram screen to which he was connected. Scientist Aiello's name got their attention. Every one of them listened attentively now.

"Well Miss Aiello, welcome to Vesuvius," I said. "I hope your visit is enlightening."

"Commander…."

"You can call me Isaac," as I smiled at her.

She smiled. "And you can call me Diana…alright, Isaac? I find it both interesting and startling, as well as exciting. There are so many questions you have answered, and yet there is so much more to learn.

"Are you hungry? We have any cuisine you may find on your planet, as well as any cuisine from our planet too."

"Actually Isaac, I am filled with too much adrenaline to eat. Can we tour your star ship?"

"Why of course, Diana, where would you like to start?"

"Do you have any laboratories on board? I am a scientist you know," as she smiled at me again.

I then stood up to help her out of her chair. My emotions were stirring, and I didn't know how forward I could, or should, get. I felt my primeval urge return as we walked out of the dining room. I already knew she was stirring too, as I monitored her emotional makeup on her hologram while she sat through the dissertation. I knew professionalism was paramount here, but I was enthralled for the first time in years. She then made it easy.

"Isaac, being a biological scientist, I was wondering if our biological makeup is the same? Do we share the same physical attributes? Do we share the same DNA? So much to ask of you."

"Diana, instead of going to a laboratory, why don't we go to my quarters to discuss this. We could be more comfortable there," I answered, not knowing the response I may illicit.

"Ok Isaac, that would be nice."

As we walked and made small talk, Diana perused the ship closely. Androids were stirring about everywhere, each with a specific task. Having a large number of androids on board made for a fewer contingent of staff, not to mention the life sustaining food and properties they needed on long voyages.

When we entered my private quarters, I dimmed the lights, allowing the cosmos to faintly illuminate the room. We were both excited to be alone for the first time, and it showed. Diana was taken back with the glass ceiling that exposed the cosmos and the neat sterile atmosphere of the room. The furniture was either white or platinum-coated, with white walls and white carpeting. I then walked toward a cabinet and asked Diana if she would care for a drink. She followed me closely and made me feel like she was studying me.

"Isaac, I've never felt so tiny. I feel much smaller than ever before, and yet I feel so protected," she said.

"There is no reason to fear anything here Diana. I know the past few days have been a traumatic experience for your people."

I felt like she was tingling as she took the glass of red wine I offered her, as she was as giddy as a school girl. Our eyes locked as we lifted our glass to each other. With a smile on my face, I placed my glass on the bar and took the glass out of her hand.

"I was wondering... is this a science experiment for you Diana?"

She smiled, "Could be, you never know, it might be bigger than that."

I smiled and cupped the back of her head in my palm and undid her bun, letting her long black hair fall against her white smock.

"You like that," she asked?

"I like you. You're beautiful."

"My nervous smile is masking the tight feeling I have in the pit of my stomach, Isaac."

I then picked her up by her waist, my large hands wrapped completely around her, and set her on the bar. Her skirt slid up as she wrapped her legs around me, and she leaned back to let me kiss her. As we kissed I felt feelings that hadn't been aroused in years. She sighed and held me closer.

"Can we walk over to the window, Isaac? I am so nervous."

I smiled and pushed a button, extending the panoramic view of the Cosmos.

"Is that okay?"

She smiled with both fear and apprehension as I then lifted her off the bar, and gently stood her on the floor. She let her skirt slide down to its normal position and slowly walked to the window, her heels accenting her body nicely. I walked over to her and put my arm around her waist as we looked at the planet Earth spinning below us.

"Wow, what a beautiful sight, spinning so slowly and yet so mysteriously. Every spin turns day into light and back again for so many people. While we are watching, people are being born and dying and we're observing it from a distance."

"Yes, time marches on. It waits for no one. That is why every moment, every encounter, is precious."

Then I turned her to me and bent over to kiss her. Her mouth was eager as we touched, with a passion that was hard to resist. The excitement we shared was growing to a crescendo as we embraced and kissed. I stopped and pulled my head back.

"Do you mind if I shower first? I've had a long day."

"Not at all."

"Have another glass of wine, I won't be long."

I then got up and went to the shower with Diana on my mind. I thought, "My God, what have I started? If word gets out about this I could lose my commission. I'll have to be completely discrete." As I washed myself and thought about the beautiful woman on the other side of the wall, I decided to throw all sheets to the wind. I was hooked.

I got dressed and walked out into my living quarters where Diana was standing at the window.

"Diana, would you like to get to know me better?"

Blushing, she didn't know what to say. She couldn't hide the thoughts that ran through her.

"Might as well, I'm already here."

We kissed again and I stopped her as she began to caress me. I was aroused and suddenly consumed with guilt. I knew this was wrong and could cost me my career.

"You feel wonderful, but I think we should stop," I said.

I then watched her walk slowly away, her sexy diminutive body gliding on the floor. "Well Isaac, today could be your lucky day," I said to myself, knowing it's been months since I've had sex…….and NEVER with an Earthling! What a beautiful sight she was. Her bronze body was glowing from the stars shining through the ceiling. I followed her again, knowing she was teasing me, but I was enchanted by her and was finding it hard to deny my carnal feelings. I bent over and rubbed my large hands across her back. She closed her eyes and gasped.

"Be gentile with me Isaac," she whispered in my ear. I kissed her and said, "Don't worry, I would never hurt you." With much anticipation, she held me tight as I laid her down on the white carpet.

"Are all Earth women as passionate as you?"

"Only Italian women, Isaac, only Italian women."

"Diana, my feelings for you are strong, but this is the wrong time and the wrong place."

"Isaac, when and how will I ever see you again?"

I stared at the cosmos and didn't answer. I then gazed down into her beautiful brown eyes and bronze skin glowing in the starlight and knew I was smitten. I knew I'd never let her go.

"Fate is cruel Diana. We are separated by a great distance, but I will find a way."

Chapter Sixteen
Khartoum

As we lay there, Diana gave me her code for her computerized watch so I can get in touch with her. As I copied it, my headband alarmed me with a message to report to the War Room. Diana rose from the bed and said she had to get back to the conference too. We both hurriedly stood up and decided to communicate later as we kissed good-bye. I arranged transportation for Diana and made my way to the round table where General Heinz and his aides were waiting.

"Commander, Khartoum has sent for reinforcements. With their location and speed, the best the reinforcements can do is nine months out. They are in another quadrant. He has not turned around either. We feel he is heading for Mars to replenish his fuel."

"Well, since he's determined to confront us, we should prepare for war. I wish we would have known this before we occupied Earth. I want your educated opinion men.

What is your thought of taking out Khartoum's ship and the two flanked on his side?" They all looked at each other for a reaction.

"Are you saying you want them terminated?" asked the General.

"That's what I'm saying. My feeling is they will turn tail when their commander and two assistants are silenced."

"You are aware you may be called before the Council for this Commander? This is an act of war."

Just then, Joshua walked in. "Have a seat Joshua, we are discussing our options regarding the Browns. How is your briefing coming?"

"I have laid out their history, it is up to them to absorb it. The videos of Atlantis and other historic scenes that played out thousands of years ago mesmerized them. I have to return soon, they are due back any minute now. Is there anything you'd like me to relate?"

"Yes Joshua," as I reached in my pocket. "I have a statement prepared that I would like you to read."

Joshua looked at it. It read, "For the last 5,000 years, we have watched the degradation of morals and ethics on your planet. It escalated 50 years ago when robots and drones took over the jobs of the working class, leaving your planet in turmoil. We have intervened at this time and have been forced to teach you the ways of the cosmos. Although good and evil exist beyond your planet, it seems your planet is ravaged more than the others. Evil is a disease that is constantly fought everywhere. Although the violent gene has been removed from our DNA, it does not prevent us from defending ourselves and being violent when the need arises, when we feel it is just. There is good and evil everywhere, and the cosmos is made up of positive and negative forces that influence everything. Yes, it even influences the cells in our body and brain."

"Isaac, you refer to good and evil in this note. Should we educate them regarding their belief in a God? I've already mentioned Moses, a figure in their Book of Knowledge."

"No, Joshua, let's not reveal everything. This visit alone will open up a can of worms, and leave their theologians gasping for answers to placate the masses. They're on the right track. They don't worship idols anymore. They know there is a creator. It's a shame that their forefathers believed we were their gods, but we must remember they were uneducated."

Joshua then stood and returned to the assembly hall. Adam and General Heinz gathered information regarding Khartoum's fleet and presented it to me. Just then the hologram lit up. President Martinez was speaking.

"Commander Glock, we would like to know when our scientists will be returned. Reports are coming in through various means stating the country is in chaos. What are your plans? When will we meet? We are hostages in our own country."

"President Martinez, I am totally aware of what's happening down there. You are not alone. The whole planet is in shock. You have to take some responsibility for what's taking place. You have hidden our existence from your people for decades. They have no semblance of reality and are in fear, fear that could have been softened. The scientists are safe and meeting as we speak. They will return with copies of what has transpired here when we are finished. There will be major changes in your text books and theological beliefs, as you are no longer alone. Hopefully you will learn from this confrontation, and your planet will experience peace for the first time in its existence." I then turned off the monitor and looked at Captain Schultz and General Heinz.

"Gentleman, are we prepared to confront Khartoum?"

"I have my reservations Commander. We may be tried for this," said General Heinz.

"Adam, what are your feelings?"

"I hate to be the deciding factor here, but I concur with you, Commander. Khartoum is a madman and will not sit by peacefully. They have too much at stake on Earth. They have been prepping their allies for dominance here for years. I think we can justify it. We must make sure everything is recorded for future consideration."

"Then it is decided. Solomon, I would like you to proceed. It is my feeling we should take out Khartoum's star ship first. If we cut the head off, the body will flounder. Do you agree?"

Chapter Seventeen
The Asteroid

Just then, the wall lit up with Science Officer Novacich speaking.

"Commander, I'm sorry to interrupt but we have an emergency. There is a giant asteroid heading for Earth. It should arrive there in 4 days, and is large enough to wipe out their civilization again. I respectfully ask your presence in the bridge."

"Thank you, Officer Novacich, I will be there shortly."

As the Hologram went off, I turned and told the table "It looks like we have a full slate."

General Heinz then spoke, "Commander, do you want to proceed with extinguishing Khartoum, or do you wish to take out his ship and the two flanking him?"

"Let's discuss this," I said. "Do you think taking out Khartoum would be enough for them to turn around? I feel it would definitely show our strength."

"Commander, I want to remind you that two of his aides, who would be next in line if he died, are commanding the ships on his flank. They may be so dogmatic as to continue because of the size of their force and to be competitive for his vacancy. Or they may simply wait for the reinforcements they called for and attack us on our exit."

"Now that is another problem. Captain, what are your feelings?"

"Commander, we have a lot at stake here. The scientists are almost done with the dissertation we gave them, and will be ready to return to Earth in a short time to share our knowledge. This alone is huge. Furthermore, we've already eliminated Khartoum's sails and now we're talking about taking out their most respected military commander in their history, as well as his aides. They have help on the way and I feel that they won't turn around. We will be forced to confront them. In addition, we have a giant asteroid on a direct collision course with Earth. Our plate is full."

"Captain Schultz and General Heinz, I have the utmost respect for both of you. This is a major decision. I would like you to alert the other 200 starship captains and relay our situation. Before we act, I would like their feelings on the matter. There is too much at stake here. We have a little time." I then went to the Bridge where Science Officer Novacich was waiting.

"Commander, thank you for coming so quickly."

"What do we have?"

"Sir, it is large, in the Ceres class. It not only will obliterate everything on Earth, but it has the capability of deflecting off and becoming another Moon. The mass is so huge, the ice has melted and differentiated enough to have a metallic core with rocky minerals in the crust."

"As a scientist, what do you believe our options are?"

"Sir, it is large and moving at approximately 25,000 mph. It has passed Mars and can reach Earth in approximately 4 days. The mass of its metallic core is too large to vaporize, even with our dark matter capabilities. We can strike a blow to it, but in doing so, it will break it into millions of pieces. It will all shower down upon Earth. Most will disintegrate in their atmosphere, but some may be large enough to cause damage."

"Can we deflect it?"

"Sir, we don't have the proper equipment onboard to perform that maneuver. This is a mother ship, not a scientific expedition. I certainly wish we did."

"What part of Earth will take the hit, Jerry?"

"It was calculated. Untouched, it would hit the area between South America and Africa in the Atlantic. It would occur in the middle of the night. A direct hit would be devastating, and if the asteroid was broken up by us, the damage would be far spread with little chance of predicting the damage. However, the sooner we break it up, the less chance of a major strike."

"It appears we have no choice. Get together with General Heinz and let's strike this as soon as possible. Because we are also in harm's way, please advise me as to its chronological timesheet, and the debris that will be large enough to sustain damage." Officer Novacich got on the intercom, paging General Heinz, and I left the bridge.

Chapter Eighteen
The Paradox

Diana returned to the assembly hall just as Joshua began to speak. When he finished reading the note I prepared, the hologram lit up with questions from the crowd.

"Ladies and Gentleman, I have completed my lecture to you today. Because major items of importance have raised their ugly head, we will not have time for a question and answer period, nor a tour of the ship. You have enough information to take back to the heads that be. We did not discuss a "creator" for various reasons. I will tell you there is a creator, and the fact we arrived and threw your beliefs into a chasm is not the answer. Your forefathers made the mistake at calling us gods years ago, and we do not want you making the same mistake. There is indeed a creator, and you will have to expand your mind. We have no intention of destroying your theological beliefs, but would like you to explore the universe peacefully. Something of great importance did come up a few minutes ago that I have an obligation to share with you. There is an asteroid heading for Earth the size of Ceres and we have less than 60 days to prepare for it."

As he spoke, a murmur from the crowd made it difficult to continue. He flashed an alert on their individual holograms for them to cease talking so he could continue.

"For this reason, we will return you to Earth as soon as possible so your grids can be turned on. We are in touch with President Martinez, and the other mother ships are in touch with the other governments they are over. Earth will be notified that if they start any hostile actions against us, they will be met with deadly force. We are turning on your power grids so you can take defensive action against the asteroid only, not for retaliatory action. We came here not to harm you, but to help and educate you. We will assist you in the destruction of this asteroid as you do not have the capability at this time. Please file out with your memory case and report to the shutter terminal for departure."

Diana looked around frantically. Her emotions were mixed. She didn't want to go back under these conditions. In fact, she didn't want to go back at all. As she walked the long portal to the shuttle hanger, her computerized watch went off.

"Diana, I want you to return to the assembly hall. We have to meet before you leave."

As she turned around, I got in my electric sled and sped towards the Hall. I entered the hall and saw her sitting there alone. We both rushed into each other's arms.

"Oh Isaac, I don't want to leave like this."

"Don't worry, I don't want you to leave either."

"What will we do? How can I stay? Where will I stay?"

Commander Davolio spoke, "As a commander, didn't you see the error of your ways at this time? Meddling emotionally and physically into the lives of an alien being is strictly prohibited, and yet you wanted to harbor her?"

"I did, Commander. As you can see by the hologram, my emotions were stirred and got the best of my better judgement. If the word "love" can be used, I think I was there."

"Commander, did you see anything unusual about her behavior at this time?"

"No Ma'am, nothing at all. I thought we were both in love, an emotion that has evaded me for years and quite frankly, it felt good."

"I'm sure by now you can see why you have been shuttled to this Institution."

Isaac hung his head and tried to review the paradox he felt himself tied. He looked at the panel, and he looked down at the wires hooked up to his body. He couldn't explain the lights going off or the dilemma he was in.

"Commander Glock, you may continue."

"Okay, where were we?"

"Commander, you were with the Earthling in the assembly hall."

"Okay. It was at this time I committed myself to being with her, and she with me. We stepped out of the hall and proceeded back to my quarters. When we got there, we kissed and I told her to make herself at home and I'd be back later. Remember, my world as I knew it was turning upside down. My plate was full."

Chapter Nineteen
The Plan

I returned to the bridge to see President Martinez on my wall.

"Commander Glock, what is happening? You did not get back to me. My country is in chaos."

"President Martinez, the whole world is in chaos. Your scientists and the others are being shuttled back to Earth as we speak. They have everything we discussed with them--everything you will need to know about your past history. We do have a problem however, a major problem. There is an asteroid heading for Earth that should arrive within 4 days. It is of the Ceres class, a very big asteroid. Your power will be returned so your scientists, and your space agency could deal with it. Our channels will be open for discussion if you like, as we have the capability to eradicate it. However, there will be collateral damage. As I said, your power grids are back. Please assess the situation and let me know what you want to do. My Science Officer Novacich will be at your disposal for updates and information in regard to its size and speed. I must add, if there is a military response of any kind to our occupation, you will be met with deadly and catastrophic force. Do I make myself clear, President Martinez?"

"I understand, Commander Glock. I will have our best minds contact you regarding this."

I then went to the war room and summoned Assistant Commander Stonecypher, General Heinz and Captain Schultz. When they arrived, we sat at the round table and summoned the other captains on the wall.

The wall then lit up. "Gentlemen, do we have a consensus on Khartoum?"

Captain Phillips, from one of the mother ships over Europe, spoke, "Sir, after conferring with the other captains, I feel I could speak for all of us. We feel you should take out Khartoum's ship only. If they don't turn around, we will still have the option for further removal if necessary. This decision was unanimous."

"Do you feel they will just hang around until their reinforcements arrive, or do you think they will they leave entirely? What is your opinion?"

"Commander, if they don't leave quickly, we feel that we should then remove the two ships flanked to his sides that contain his assistants, and we feel we should do this instantly. Shock and awe is all they understand. We have to put fear in them. They have to see the might of our new weapon and know they'll have no chance in a confrontation."

"Okay, it is decided. Solomon, get in contact with the 100 ships en route to Mars. Tell them to have one of their ships eradicate Khartoum's ship immediately. Have them eavesdrop on his two flanking ships and eradicate them if they don't turn around. The attack should be immediate and decisive. I only want three ships to get involved. I don't want to drain our dark matter in case we have a confrontation later. I will need your visual attack on my screen and a follow-up when completed. We may have to act further. Have them remain in Code Brown-Defcon-3. Contact me when they are terminated."

Chapter Twenty
Diana

I had to get back to Diana. As I entered my quarters, I saw her lying on the bed gazing at the cosmos. She jumped up and rushed to me, giving me a kiss.

"Oh Isaac, what will we do?"
"I don't know. I'll figure something out. At the moment, I am confronted with two emergency situations and a planet that is in disarray."

I knew I shouldn't divulge anything but the pressure I was under demanded a release valve.

I looked her in the eye, "Not only do we have a life-ending asteroid headed this way, but we are being trailed by our biggest adversary, the Browns."

"The Browns? The same Browns who occupied Egypt and the Middle East thousands of years ago? The same Browns Joshua schooled us on?"

"Yes, the same. They are intervening in our mission and we will have to use military action against them to stop them. We've already tried to reason with them. They are six days out at the moment."

"Oh my, what will you do?"

"We are going to have to eliminate their Commander and his subordinates. We will use a shock and awe campaign to turn them around. We are outnumbered, and they have reinforcements on the way. We have no other choice."

"How will you do that, Isaac, being outnumbered?"

"Diana, we have the most advanced weapon system in the universe. We have controlled dark matter and can strike from great distances. We can even be selective with our strikes and take out what we want."

"Being involved in the scientific community, I am quite aware of dark matter. They have been trying to harness its energy since the first part of the 21st century. I'm from Italy, and our neighbor Switzerland has had an atom splitter there for years. How did you do it?"

"It's very complicated, and being you're a Biological Nuclear Scientist it may be difficult for you to comprehend. Let's just say the answer is in the nuclear plasma and particles such as the axion and neutralino, which are part of weakly interacting massive particles, otherwise known as WIMPs. Their mass isn't as dense as "ordinary" particles, which comprise only 5 % of all the mass in the universe. Dark energy and dark matter, on the other hand, comprise 95 % of all the matter in the universe. The trick is we learned how to harness it. Your famous scientist, Einstein, wasn't far off in his Theory of Relativity."

Judge Lisko interrupted, "Commander, were you aware at the time you were divulging vital military and scientific secrets, or were you so smitten you didn't care?"

"I have to say I was aware of what I was doing but didn't think she had the capability of understanding it. In my mind, she had to be a nuclear physicist to put it together. Like I said earlier, I was under attack from various sources and I needed to vent."

"Don't you believe your assistant or captain would have been a more appropriate outlet?"

"I do now."

"Continue please," said Judge Lisko.

"Diana appeared to be very interested in what I was saying and started to ask more questions. I stopped her and grabbed her shoulders and looked into her eyes."

"What about me Isaac, what will you do with me?"

"You are indeed an enigma. I haven't decided how to handle our situation. All I know is I care about you and want you in my life. I'd like you to go with me. I don't ever want to be away from you."

"Oh Isaac, are you saying you want to marry me? Is marriage possible?"

"We are aware of the pact you call marriage. We call it a union contract, when two people unite as one and vow through a contract to be one forever."

"is that possible Isaac? Are interstellar unions possible?"

"It is against the laws of the cosmos, Diana. Our DNA molecules do not line up entirely. In the past, some strange beings were created by mixing the double helix. It would be possible if you were cleansed of your eggs. You would not be able to reproduce."

I then lifted her off the ground and kissed her passionately. Her fingernails tore into me as I put her on the bed, still embracing. As our passion ripped apart my ethics, we made love under the stars.

Chapter Twenty-One
Security Breach

As we lay there talking, my alarm went off, paging me to the war room. I told Diana to remain here while I was gone. When I reached the war room, General Heinz, Captain Schultz and Assistant Commander Stonecypher were seated at the round table looking grim. The hologram wall was lit and ready for use.

"What's the matter? You look disturbed?" I said.

"Commander, it appeared Khartoum was warned somehow of the attack and took evasive maneuvers, diverting off the course his fleet was traveling. We eavesdropped on his ship, but they garbled the communication, making it hard to decipher. He cloaked his ship but we found him. He is now extinguished. Here is a video of his destruction."

I stared at the screen and thought about what he said. "How could he have known of the attack?" I wondered.

"Joshua, is it possible he eavesdropped on us?"

"Sir, for him to eavesdrop, he would have to have some knowledge of dark matter. And if that's the case, he has been eavesdropping on us for a while. However, I do not believe he has that capability. If he did, he would have known of our intention to remove his sails, and it appeared he didn't, as there were no defensive maneuvers at the time."

"You're right, Joshua. Adam, do you have any thoughts on this matter?"

"I'm currently at a loss for words, Isaac. If there is a mole, it's one of us, unless one of us discussed it with someone else. We were the only ones who were privy to this information."

To a man, they all denied conversing about it. And then it hit me, I did mention it to Diane. "But how could that be?" I thought to myself.

Suddenly the wall lit up, flashing a message in red. "Code Three, Alert, Alert, Alert, we have reason to believe an Earthling is still on the ship. I repeat, Alert, Alert, Alert, we have reason to believe an Earthling is still on the ship. All security personnel please report to the Bridge."

Captain Schultz appeared on the wall. "What is going on?"

"Captain, there was one Earthling not accounted for when transports were counted. All shuttles have departed with one Earthling not accounted for. According to reports, it is the scientist from Italy, Diana Aiello."

"How could this have happened? Have you checked the obvious places? Have you retraced her steps?"

"Yes Sir. We checked all areas between the hanger and the assembly hall, and checked the dining room area also. One of our personnel believes he saw her with Commander Glock."

Captain Schultz cleared the wall and looked at me.

"Isaac, when was the last time you saw her? Do you have any idea where she may be?"

"The last time I saw her, she was heading for the dining room. I instructed her on how to get there. That must have been ninety minutes ago, more or less. I think we better get to the bridge."

We all got up and proceeded to the bridge. I decided I had to go to my room to check on her.

"Gentleman, I am stopping at my quarters for a minute. I'll be along shortly. Have all areas checked closely."

I opened my door and found her on the bed again staring at the cosmos.

"Isaac, I could never get used to this view, it changes every hour."

I walked over to the bed and leaned over and gently kissed her. She pulled me down on her.

"Oh Isaac, I missed you. What are we going to do? I'm sure they already know I'm missing."

I sat up on the edge of the bed and looked her in the eye. I felt love for the first time in years and was confused, terribly confused.

"Diana, they do know you're missing and they are searching the ship as we speak. With our technology, it's only a matter of time before you're discovered. I'm going to have to take you back. It's better this way for both of us."

"What if I tell them I don't want to go back? What if I tell them I'm afraid of the asteroid and afraid I might die, and you were the only one who could help me? I could tell them I'd be of help to them if they wanted to study human beings. After all, I am a Bio-Nuclear Scientist."

I looked at her and she seemed so frail, so small, and yet so beautiful. I felt like I had to help her somehow, and I knew I had to help myself out of this predicament I created. I tried to reason with the emotions that were flooding me. She got up and walked around the room, talking as she walked. I heard her and I didn't hear her. My head was spinning.

Chapter Twenty-Two

A Perfect Storm

Then my alarm went off, summoning me to the bridge. We were in Code Three.

"Commander, we have a major problem. The Browns reinforcements have traversed a wormhole and can arrive in 3 days without Khartoum's armada, unless they wait and arrive together."

"I'll be right there!"

"Isaac, what will you do? How will you stop them?" Asked Diana as she walked up to me.

"This situation is getting out of control now. We're going to have to use our military advantage over them, and yet I don't know if it'll be enough. Stay here until I get back, okay?"

"I'm afraid, Isaac. I'm afraid for you and me. I think I'm falling in love with you and our world is falling apart."

I lifted her up and held her close to me. As the smell of her perfume mesmerized me, I ran my fingers through her hair and pulled her head back so I could look into her beautiful brown eyes. She was beautiful and I knew I was in love too.

Then I removed my equipment belt and went into my closet to change my uniform. When I came back, she was in bed calling me over to her in a low whisper.

"Damn, you look beautiful in the starlight," I said.

"Isaac, you're dressed for work, can't you stay for a while? She smiled and bit her lip. "I'll make it worth your while."

I was tempted to stay a while, but I knew I shouldn't. I had fish to fry.

Reluctantly, I said, "Diana I have to go. I'll be back soon. You just stay right here."

We kissed and I left my quarters and headed for the bridge. As I passed the hanger, I saw our fleet of nuclear saucers hovering above the floor, ready for use. I paused and reflected on the war games we played at Galactic Headquarters, and reflected on how much power we carried. I knew our only chance was a quick and surprise attack, as we will be outnumbered four to one.

I entered the bridge, which was a large circular room with androids working computer screens. It had an eerie glow tonight from the screens and the cosmos glowing overhead. Adam, Solomon and Joshua were waiting. We had been together through many campaigns and I totally trusted their judgement. When they saw my entrance, they turned on the wall.

"Gentlemen, what do we have?"

"Isaac, the Brown's reinforcements have successfully traversed a large wormhole and took six months off their arrival time. If they don't wait for Khartoum's armada they can be here in three days. If they come together they'll be here in six days."

"What model ship do their reinforcements have Solomon?"

"Commander Hotep is using the new SS-5000, while his fleet consists of the SS-4000. They number less than 100 starships."

"Have we eavesdropped on Hotep?"

Solomon's android spoke, "We have, Sir, and they are preparing for war. They will strike in two waves. Hotep's armada will arrive in 3 days, with Khartoum's armada arriving in 6 days. They will be coming after your ship first, Commander."

I then sat down at the table and joined them.

"Thank you. Please keep us posted of their whereabouts and any changes they make."

"Gentleman, we will have a confrontation in 3 days or less, an asteroid strike in 4 days, and a second assault in 6 days. I think we could coordinate an attack simultaneously on all three. If they are coming here for me, we can also use the debris from the asteroid strike to disrupt their attack by letting it rain down on them. If they want to be in America, have Officer Novacich calculate the exact time the asteroid can be hit so that the debris can rain down on them. Adam, contact every mother ship's captain, and have them on my wall in one hour. Solomon, contact our ships en route to Mars, and have them take out Khartoum's aides' ships immediately. Also, have your military aides from our mother ships devise a plan of action for our impending attack that we will review. I would like that in two hours. Then recall our ships from their mission to Mars, and have them stand by at an elevation of 200 miles over the planet. We will have 100 ships at 200 miles out and 100 ships on Earth. Get President Martinez on the air."

The wall then lit up with President Martinez sitting in the Oval Office with his top aides.

"Good evening, President Martinez. Your scientists have been returned to you and I'm quite sure you have reviewed the copy of our dissertation. We will meet tomorrow morning at your Pentagon building regarding the disarming of your nuclear weapons and their means of transporting them. You will not be at a military disadvantage against your foes, as the whole planet will be disarmed. It is time for you to live in peace and use nuclear energy for more productive means. If you do not, we will be back. Contact your scientists and let them know we will be exploding the asteroid headed for you in approximately 4 days. There won't be a significant life-ending event, but a meteor shower, if you will, with little collateral damage. We cannot predict loss of life, although it may be minimal at best. I don't intend to be rude, but at the moment, I don't have time for questions. I advise you to study the information brought back to you. We will land on the lawn of your Pentagon building tomorrow at 7 AM. Thank you."

We then ordered some caffeine because it looked like it was going to be a long night. After discussing our status for a while, the wall lit up with Captain Phillips speaking.

"Commander Glock, General Heinz, Captain Schultz, to a man, the mother ship's captains are in agreement a pre-eminent strike is in order. Sir, we have 1,000 saucers on each ship, and we have 200 ships. That equates to 200,000 saucers plus 200 mother ships with a technology superior to them. The first volley will come from Hotep, of which 99 of his ships have inferior military technology. The choice is yours. We could ambush them from the dark side of the Moon or just go get them. We have the technology to eradicate them from our present position without losing any saucers from their lasers. We also feel if we eradicate them, Khartoum's armada will turn around too."

I then asked General Heinz for his suggestions.

"Solomon, what are your ideas on this situation? Do you agree with Captain Phillips and the fleet?"

"Isaac, this is a delicate situation. If all goes to plan, we would remove most of their armada. We've already exterminated

Khartoum and we're going to have to go before the Galactic Council for that alone. Furthermore, if we allow them to get close, and we fight them over Earth, our fallacy of spreading peace in the galaxy will become a myth. First of all, I suggest we take out the asteroid as soon as possible. Our new weapon system is so powerful, we don't have to rely on the asteroid's debris hitting or missing them. Furthermore, if we act now, Earth will be spared a catastrophe, and we will be looked upon as heroes, or perhaps God as we were in the past. And, it is highly possible that if we take out Hotep's ship and his assistants, they may run and fight another day."

"Do we really want them to fight another day Solomon?"

"Isaac, I am thinking about the ramifications of our act to the Galactic Council. We already will be called on the carpet for Khartoum."

The wall then lit up with Colonel Barbb from the Bridge speaking.

"Commander, Hotep and the two ships on his flank just dropped back to the middle of the pack. It appears to be an evasive maneuver."

"Thank you, Colonel."

I then looked at my staff with a confused look on my face. I found it interesting Hotep decided to hide while we talked about him.

"Adam, they don't have eavesdropping capabilities, do they? I find their move highly coincidental."

"No Sir. They haven't that capability yet."

I sat there, staring at the wall and tried to put these events into perspective.

"Gentleman, it is late. Let's sleep on this and return here at 0500 hours. I've already directed Officer Novacich to destroy the asteroid. Adam, please get in touch with him and let me know when he'll have the coordinates for its destruction. Goodnight."

Chapter Twenty-Three
The Discovery

As I spoke, the panel stirred, each one wanting to speak. Military Adjunct spoke first.

"Commander, did you realize the consequences of your military plan?"

"I did Sir, but I was trying to survive here. We were to be under attack from two armadas who wanted nothing less than to put my feather in their cap."

"Are you aware you attacked them first, Commander?" asked Judge Lisko.

"I am Ma'am, but explained that earlier. Knowing their history, they were not coming here for peace, but to destroy us so their factions on Earth would remain powerful."

"And the fact the Browns knew your intentions before you did… didn't that make you wonder what was transpiring?" asked Commander Davolio.

"Not at the time, Ma'am."

"We need more information. Continue please."

I returned to my quarters and found Diana asleep. I quietly removed my uniform and stood there admiring her tanned petite body lying there, illuminated by the stars above. I walked up to her side of the bed and sat down, caressing her ever so easily. She murmured as I ran my hands across her beautiful nude body, arousing her erect nipples. She awoke and smiled at me, her olive eyes glistening in the starlight. She grabbed my neck and pulled herself up to me. Our mouths locked as she sucked on my tongue and my hands caressed her smooth skin. She moaned as I laid her back down and kissed the inside of her thighs. Just as I was......

Suddenly the door burst open and six armed guards rushed in, lasers drawn. Diane grabbed the covers as I jumped to my feet, grabbing a sheet.

"Commander, you'll have to come with me. There's been a breach of security and the signal leads to your quarters. I assume this is Scientist Ionna? We have been looking for her as well."

I stood there, embarrassed and dumbfounded.

"What do you mean, the signal leads to my quarters? I am the Commander here. Why wasn't I notified of this?"

"Sir, we traced the signal from here to the War Room and back again. The Chief of Security demanded we follow the signal and eradicate it. I'm afraid you both are going to have to come with me."

We then got dressed and our arms were anesthetized for security reasons. We were then led to Security Headquarters and placed in two separate rooms. We sat alone for over an hour. All the while my head was racing, reviewing the incidents in my mind that led up to this. And then Captain Schultz walked in my room.

Chapter Twenty-Four
Imprisoned

"Adam, what is the meaning of this? What's going on?"

"Sir, our sensors have been detecting a rogue signal on the ship for the last several hours. Once we located it, we started following it. It initially started in the assembly hall and then went to the dining room. From there, it went to your quarters, to the war room, and back to your quarters. Sir, I think you've been compromised."

I looked at him in amazement as I reflected on my day's activities.

"What kind of signal, Adam?"

"Sir, everything you talked about was relayed to the Browns--everything."

"What kind of device was it?"

"It was a watch that doubled as a camera and video recorder. We located it in your equipment belt."

"A watch! My equipment belt? How could that be?"

"Sir, we believe Scientist Aiello placed it there since it initially began in the assembly hall and ended in your room where she was also found. She is being interrogated as we speak."

I scratched my head and thought about what transpired today, and the thoughts I shared with Diana, and how the Browns reacted simultaneously with my directions in the war room. But Diana? No, it couldn't be," I thought."

"Adam, are you sure? Is it possible it was planted on her by someone else?"

"Sir, if that were true, how did it get in your belt?"

"Can I see her Adam? I'd like to talk to her. I can't believe this transpired."

"Sir, you are currently under arrest for collaborating with an Earthling. There are rules I have to follow. I'm sure you understand. Your knowledge of the device will be investigated, as well as your familiarity with the Earthling. I'm sorry."

"Our mission, Adam, what about the Browns? Have you eliminated Hotep and his subordinates?"

"Not yet sir. We were to meet in the morning before your meeting with President Martinez. Because of your current situation, you have been relieved of your command pending an investigation, and we can't discuss this. Assistant Commander Stonecypher is in command now, and is in the war room meeting with General Heinz as we speak. We have been able to play back all data that was recorded and sent to the Browns. I'm sorry this happened Sir. "Can you follow me to your holding quarters?"

I followed Capt. Schultz to my new quarters in the aft of the ship. It was in stark comparison to my living quarters. It was essentially a room with a bathroom and bed. It was an ugly gray and there was no window. There was a camera in the ceiling that observed my every move. I was told I had to stay there until I was transported to the correctional facility for evaluation.

I was fed three times a day and had time to think about what had transpired, plenty of time. I couldn't believe I was duped. I wondered how Diana was doing and what she was going through.

I wondered about our upcoming skirmish with the Browns, and the asteroid that was heading for Earth. I wondered if any large fragments would do damage upon entering their atmosphere. I wondered if the meeting with President Martinez would go well. I thought about a lot of things.

But mostly, I sat there and thought about Diana and the love I lost. We all are confronted with the loss of a loved one in our lives and I don't know which is worse, an actual death where finality seals fate, or a torn love affair where the thought of her existing out of your reach haunts you on a daily basis. Or maybe it was missing her smile and larger than life attitude that once brought joy to a complex man. The room she entered in my mind will always have an emptiness to it now. What once was filled with joy and the promise of a new tomorrow now holds a scar to that part of my brain that bled after she left. The pragmatist in me looked at reality and said it happened for the best. The dreamer in me wanted a new tomorrow. Such is the paradox in which I dwell.

Chapter Twenty-Five
The Questioning

Days went by and it came time for my shuttle to the Galactic Floating Correctional Facility. I was told nothing of Diana's fate and it tore me up inside. I was transported by a cyborg in a saucer. I was incapacitated with pharmaceutical injections for the journey that would take eighteen months of Earth time, essentially placed in a coma.

Psychiatrist Gilmore then asked, "Commander, did you have any knowledge of Scientist Aiello's motives at this time?"

"No Ma'am, I didn't. I was blindsided by it all. It was like a sucker punch in the gut. I really cared about her and although I knew it was wrong, I felt there could be a future someday. Even though she was an Earthling, we seemed to share the same ideals and hit it off so easily. Sometimes we would say the same thing at the same time. It was amazing and refreshing speaking to someone with my intelligence. We would bounce things off each other with quick wit. Although we seemed to be very compatible, it seems like a mirage now, blurry from a distance but clearer when you close in."

"Are you really saying this Earthling was on the same level as you intellectually?"

"I am, Dr. Gilmore. After all, she was a descendant of the Roman Empire we genetically altered, and she was a nuclear biologist with a high IQ."

Commander Davolio chimed in, "Commander, are you saying you were blindsided by this woman? What do you mean?"

"I am. I'm saying I was smitten. I can't explain it. I don't know why or how it happened, but I lost control of my senses and threw all sheets to the wind."

"I can assure you when this conversation is completed, you will know why and how she was selected by the Browns," said Psychiatrist Gilmore, as she coyly smiled.

Galactic Judge Lisko and Galactic Theologian Peloza stared at me and typed some notes into their recorders as the wall lit up with my vital signs going through the roof.

"Commander, are you saying you felt love for this Earthling?" asked Judge Lisko.

"Yes, that's what I'm saying, a feeling I haven't felt for years. For some reason, the computer chip that hid emotions was overridden. I can't explain it. I felt as if I was a teenager again, before the chip was installed."

"And you were aware that genetically the Earthling's biological makeup consisted of 26 chromosomes, whereas ours are 28 and reproduction in the normal sense was impossible?"

"Theologian Peloza, reproduction did not enter the fray. It was a charismatic and visceral attraction. Her personality simply took over where mine left off. Offspring was never discussed. It started off as pure lust and evolved."

Suddenly I felt bombarded, and the wall disclosed that fact. I was getting hit from all sides of my psyche and it was lit up like Galactic Independence Day.

"Commander, you are aware, as a commander, the computer chip that was installed in you prevented you from feeling emotions and personal attachments," replied Science Officer Novacich.

"I am aware of that, Sir."

"Realizing that, do you have any explanation for what happened? Do you have any idea how you could have been compromised?"

"Again sir, all I can tell you is it was a visceral reaction I haven't felt in years. Do you yourself have any explanation for this?"

The panel all looked at each other as they watched the wall.

"Commander," said Judge Lisko, "according to our diagnostics, you have been very forthcoming in all that we have asked. But we have one more question for you."

The Council looked at me in unison and then looked at Judge Lisko.

"Commander, you say Scientist Aiello's IQ was on a level with yours. Do you feel she would be of any use to the scientists on our planet?"

As they looked at the wall for my reaction, I wondered why are they asking me this? I was puzzled by the question. Are they inferring she is still locked up somewhere and wasn't allowed to return to Earth? Are they thinking of perhaps utilizing her? Are they testing my devotion to her? My mind rambled as I thought of many things, and then... I thought of her again.

"Commander, did you hear the question?"

"Excuse me. What was the question again?"

"Commander, do you feel Scientist Aiello would be beneficial to our scientists?"

"She is a nuclear biologist with great knowledge of human beings from planet Earth. Since we don't inhabit Earth, I think she would be of use in that manner, yes. In other words, if we are truly serious in studying different species in the galaxy," I said.

Chapter Twenty-Six

Compromised

"Commander, what if I told you we have Scientist Aiello in an adjoining room being questioned as we speak?"

The wall lit up again as my physiological sensors went crazy. "How is this possible," I thought?

"I'm finding that hard to believe. If she was in custody, it would be natural for her to be held hostage on the Vesuvius, not here."

"Commander, we did extensive physiological and psychological tests on her and decided she needed deciphering that only an institution like this affords," added Dr. Gilmore.

"Deciphering? What are you saying? You are saying she's here!"

"Sir, we discovered that the Browns did extensive research into your genetic and sociological background, and searched for the type of woman that is attractive to you. By eavesdropping at base headquarters, they knew of your pending trip and your arrival.

Because of the distance between you and Earth, they got there as quickly as they could. They then had androids select Dr. Aiello, as she was a noted scientist and would be chosen for your mission. They then hypnotized her with the newly discovered drug Marathon. They purposely boarded androids in front of her, knowing they would be stopped and her chances of boarding wouldn't be scrutinized, basically allowing her in without detection. Being she was psychologically altered, without a chip of any kind, made her undetectable to your screening when she boarded. The rest was up to you. You responded to her just like they knew you would, even to her small talk and bantering. Her unconscious goal was to seduce you and record your conversations."

The wall lit up again and stayed lit. My emotions went off the charts. I had questions to ask but didn't know where to start.

"Dr. Gilmore, are you saying this was an unconscious act by her, that she was psychologically induced and had no control over her actions?"

"I am Commander, but there is more. By psychologically screening her, we discovered the love emotion she felt for you was indeed real. She essentially trumped the drug and fell in love with you on her own accord. As time transpired, her emotions took over and essentially overcame the drug. Apparently, the Browns didn't take into account the virility of the Mediterranean people."

"Where is she? What is her fate?"

"Commander, we can't take her back to Earth. She knows too much now. Furthermore, she would probably be ostracized by her colleagues. We have decided to send her back to Hercules to let her blend into our scientific community," stated Galactic Theologian Peloza.

"Where is she now? Is she really in an adjoining room," I nervously asked?

"She is, Commander, and we're going to let you see her, but we feel you shouldn't see each other until your chip is repaired," said Judge Lisko. "The fact remains your chip was compromised by the Browns and it is in need of repair. You were susceptible to your genetic makeup and this has to be corrected, or quite simply, it may happen again. It may compromise other commanders in the future, as they have the same security chip. This flaw has to be detected and fixed."

"Regarding this fact, Commander," added Judge Lisko, we don't find Scientist Aiello guilty of a crime, as she was psychologically altered. We also don't find you responsible in this matter, as it is evident your chip was compromised."

"I have to ask... If this was a flaw in the chip and I was compromised without my own feelings and emotions, will I still feel the same about her as I do now when my chip is "repaired"?

"Probably not, Commander," said Dr. Gilmore. "She will look no different to you than an android. The emotion "love" will not enter into your mind again. You're not a young man anymore, and there is no need to be distracted from your mission. Your energy will only be directed for the good of the Galactic Air Force."

"Okay," said Judge Lisko, "I propose we adjourn to tomorrow morning. This has been a long day."

CHAPTER TWENTY-SEVEN
Emptiness

The panel left the room, leaving me to look around, taking everything in while I waited for my escorts. "How could I escape from here?" I thought. The room I sat in was cold and icy gray in color, with a stainless-steel chair for me to sit in. The panel sat above me on an elevated level, surrounded by a large desk in a semi-circular design. The floor consisted of gray tile, and there were no windows. The wall was lit and I knew it was still recording my emotions, even though the panel left the room. I knew I could fly any saucer on this ship, but how would I get to them with anesthetized arms. How could I get to them anyway, with each door in this facility needing an iris identification to enter?

I recapped the day's activities. "Okay Isaac," I said to myself, "there will be no charges for co-mingling with an Earthling, and Diana is supposedly in the next room. My chip is going to be repaired, and I'll look at her again as if she was a bowl of soup.

And if that isn't good enough, I still have charges against me. What else can happen?"

I waited. Tea was brought to me by an android and I was fed with a straw. It didn't take long before two androids entered for my return to my room.

The night was long. Thinking about the day's events and the information I learned today was staggering, to say the least. But thinking about Diana being on the same ship with me made for a sleepless night. Where was she? Was she in an adjoining room or was she sequestered?

"Okay," I said to myself, "let's get organized. She will be set free on Vesuvius to continue her occupation. I will not be charged for co-mingling with her. My chip will be repaired and I would feel the same about her as I feel about eating lunch-- wonderful!!! And I still have to face the music for Khartoum and his armada. What will they do to me?"

After a restless night, I was awakened by music on the room's speaker at 0600 hours. Two androids then entered my room with food and caffeine beverages. I was escorted to my shower where I just stood there while blasts of water hit me from all directions, my arms still at my side. I walked through an air dryer with hot air that dried me off almost instantly. The whole process took less than two minutes. They clothed me and we walked the long walk to the Galactic Council chambers. I felt like a criminal as we passed others with their stares. They took me inside, and sat me at my chair in front of the panel's large desk. I sat and waited.

They soon filed in and as they took their seats, I studied each one individually. Though scientifically sound and highly educated, only one member had ever served on a mother ship in a military capacity, that being former Commander Davolio. Military Adjunct Ross was a general, albeit, but he was a lawyer. Davolio was the first of a few woman commanders that would serve, and had demonstrated great leadership skills under fire. I felt I should try to get on her better side as the questioning began.

"Commander Glock, we still have the matter of the Browns to which to contend." General Ross stated. "I'm sure you were aware you broke law after law numerous times as you continued your mission."

"I was aware of the laws, Sir, but with all due respect, there is only one flight commander amongst you. I'm quite sure Commander Davolio can attest that situations arise running a mother ship that are beyond the rules of laws and regulations established. It is then that your experience comes into play."

Commander Davolio replied, "Commander, you've stated the reason you first disabled the Browns sails was to slow them down. The implications you suggested were founded on what grounds and were they discussed with your staff?"

"Yes, Commander Davolio, we discussed the ramifications both for and against disabling their sails for hours. It was discussed in our war room and was given much credence. Because of Commander Khartoum's past war mongering and the size of his fleet at the moment, we felt we were given no choice but to disable his armada. We also felt if he knew we could disable him at such a distance, he may not want to continue. It was a deterrent to war. The history of the Browns was not one of peace, but of Galactic dominance, and we felt they didn't come in peace. On the other hand, our mission to Number Three was one of peace, designed to keep nuclear weapons out of space and to educate them regarding their past history. Because of the many cataclysmic occurrences on their planet, most of their history has been erased. It is only their 5-7,000 years they have knowledge of. We wanted to instill in them the fact they are not new to the universe, and other highly technological civilizations existed in the past. Essentially, we wanted to humble them and make them think of their future."

Then I added, "Members of the Council, I would like to ask you some questions too. I was plucked from my ship in the middle of a mission, a mission that, as it turned out, carried with it grave consequences. I would like to know what transpired after I left. Was the asteroid effectively destroyed? Was Khartoum and Hotep's fleet immobilized or was there a war? Were the nuclear warheads on Number Three destroyed? Did the Earthlings want to live in peace after their education? This is the situation when you removed me! This is what I faced."

"Commander, those are good questions. I can assure you when you leave here today each one of them will be answered," Judge Lisko assured.

Theologian Peloza then looked me in the eye and asked, "Commander, I'd like to know who gave you the clearance to "educate" the Earthlings on their past history?"

"Dr. Peloza, that order came from Base Command at Base Headquarters. They felt that if the Earthlings had knowledge of their previous civilizations being erased, they might be more cautious in the future."

"The subject of God entered your dissertation to them. Don't you feel like you were upsetting the apple cart there? Do you really think it was your business to talk about God and a higher power when their whole civilization revolves around that subject?"

"I was aware of all of that. I also was aware that they revered us in the past of being their gods. I wanted to make it clear there is a higher power and it wasn't us. The only thing they will have to substantiate in their minds is the fact they are not alone in this universe. They had thought they were for thousands of years."

CHAPTER TWENTY-EIGHT
Absolvement

After a thirty-minute break, the panel returned to the room.

"Commander, you had many questions. We will try to answer them for you, as you have been honest and direct with us," said Judge Lisko.

Science Officer Novacich then spoke, "Commander, regarding the asteroid, it was broken up at a distance from Number Three by lasers fired by Commander Phillips and Commander Maro. There was no damage to Number Three as some were deflected from Number Three's path, and the remaining pieces disintegrated in their atmosphere. This event was minor compared to why you are here to stand trial."

"Commander, General Ross and I have studied your military response to Commander Khartoum. We, as a Council, have ruled on your decision against the Browns. But before we go there, let me fill you in on what happened after you were relieved of your duties", said Judge Lisko.

"Your decision to locate and destroy Commander Khartoum and his two aides was carried out per your orders. Commander Hotep was then made aware of their destruction and decided to hide his ship in the middle of his armada while they decided how to retaliate. After some communication between Khartoum's fleet and his, they all decided to proceed to Number Three in waves, hoping to get closer before they struck back.

The 100 star ships you sent to hover at 200 miles above Number Three commanded by Commander Phillips did not take any aggressive action per directives from Asst. Commander Stonecypher. Per your eavesdropping capability, Commander Phillips intercepted a message from Commander Hotep to Galactic Headquarters, stating they were turning around and were pressing charges against you, Commander Glock. They reported their destruction to the Galactic Council Headquarters, along with the fact that Khartoum was there to observe only and never showed aggression to you or your fleet. They also stated they were in awe of your new military capabilities and needed more information before striking back.

Commander Glock, we have heard your version of what took place, along with your reasoning of why you took action against Commander Khartoum. The military strategy part of your "chip" is being diagnosed as we speak. We already know the emotional sequence was over-ridden and is need of repair. This segment may have crossed over and created the paranoia you displayed against Commander Khartoum. Regardless, Commander Khartoum and his two aides are dead, along with their crew mates, not to mention the cost of three star ships. You could have created a grave situation, putting the lives of many at stake.

However, after going through the records of the surviving star ships of Commander Khartoum's fleet, we discovered that he indeed was there to attack you, and had been in touch with Commander Hotep regarding an attack on you previous to his communication with you. Before they were detected, they essentially were going to ambush you before you left their solar system. How you came to the conclusion to take action before he did, without his provocation, is a mystery to us.

So, what we have here is a commander taking offensive action against another force without provocation. The fact you were correct in the long run will be taken into account, as it appears you actually were saving lives. We also feel by you taking action the way you did, you might have averted a war.

Therefore, we as a council agree, you will not be held liable for your actions. However, you will not command another star ship either. Your chip will be repaired and you will be confined to Star Ship Command for duties that they may see fit. With your experience, Commander Glock, you may be a Wartime Commander instructor at the Stellar Academy."

"Members of the Panel, I am trying to digest your reasoning here. What happened to our initial mission to remove nuclear weapons on Number Three, and their instructions for peacetime use of nuclear energy?"

"Commander, because of the time that elapsed since you left Number Three and now, a lot has taken place there. Yes, Asst.

Commander was successful in disarming the Earthlings, but because of the advent of cyborgs and automated equipment, Number Three has become a war zone. The affluent now live in armed camps, while the masses roam the streets without food, jobs or a home. Industrialization and high wages led to mass unemployment and political unrest. The situation there is similar to our planet before the extermination of weak species, and technical education took place. The fact that you removed the nuclear weapons when you did probably saved millions of lives."

I listened in shock to this news, and at the same time, I felt a sense of relief that Diana wasn't on the planet any longer.

Chapter Twenty-Nine
The Virus

"Members of the panel, what if I refuse to have my chip repaired?" I asked as I gasped, grabbed my chest and coughed

"What if I step down from Government Service and sail into the sunset, so to speak? What if I tell you that I liked the rush I had when Scientist Aiello and I were enrapt, and would like to continue the relationship?" I said in great pain, coughing again.

"Commander, are you okay? You seem to have trouble breathing.

"I'm fine," I said. "It must be nerves."

"Commander, what if I told you, you never made love to Scientist Aiello? What if I told you, yes, you kissed, but the cerebral part of your chip refrained you from sexual contact? Yes, she was in your quarters, and yes you kissed, but your emotions caused your damaged chip to influence you in believing your relationship was consummated. She has been thoroughly briefed and examined as well, and there was no sexual contact between you, just kissing and elevated vital signs. However, for some reason, she did fall in love with you and you with her. We can't explain this at the moment."

I sat there in amazement and stared at them. "What are they talking about?" I wondered. "That can't be true. I can still smell her beautiful perfume and feel her touch."

"The fact remains, you are an important part of our Interstellar Space Program, perhaps our finest stellar officer in history. I might add that this fact was taken into account when your case was reviewed. For you to step down would be a disservice to your fellow comrades and to your family that served before you. Are you saying you would give up your career for this woman, Commander Glock?" asked Judge Lisko.

I was getting weaker as she spoke. I then coughed violently and slumped over in my chair, the oxygen mask falling from my face as I slowly slid to the floor. I was conscious as I was carried to a hospital bed on a gurney by medics. I soon passed out from hyperventilating due to the coughing and the pain in my chest. When I came to, I was staring at the cosmos above me and breathing heavily into a machine. I was hooked up intravenously, and the hologram wall in front of me was recording my physical statistics. I felt weak and longed for Diana.

"Oh, to see her again," I thought. "Where can she be?" I wondered.

Dr. Brewer walked in wearing a white suit with a mask. He touched the "wall" searching for statistics regarding my condition and turned toward to me.

"Commander, can you understand me? Do you hear me?"

I nodded that I did.

"Commander, as you know, you have contracted a human virus that is gradually eating away at your chromosomes. The last time we confronted this issue was over two thousand years ago when we assisted the Romans. Since then we have tried to combat it with various anti-virus medication to no avail. The virus is alive and well. But we have new techniques that are being tested as we speak. We have the Earthling in Isolation and we are extracting fluids from her searching for an antibody."

I raised the mask off my mouth. "Can I see her?" I asked."

"Not at the moment, Commander. Like I said, she is in Isolation."

I raised the mask from my face and pleaded.

"Dr. Brewer, I am already infected by this virus." I grabbed my chest and gasped again. "What harm would it do if we occupied the same room in separate beds? You see, I love her and am afraid I may not see her again."

Dr. Brewer looked at me and stared at the wall. He touched the wall again looking for any information that would be encouraging.

"First of all, if you don't put that mask on and leave it alone, I'll be forced to sedate your arms again. Regarding your request, I will take it up with my associates and get back to you. I don't want you speaking. You need to rest. This virus is moving very fast as noted by your blood tests. Please relax and I'll get back to you."

I nodded and he walked off.

Chapter Thirty
Gloom

The room was lit by the soft, faint light of the cosmos. While I stared at the stars in the distance, the door to my room opened and Diana walked in, closing the door behind her. She walked up to me, removed the mask from my face, and bent over to kiss me on my forehead. I was shocked to see her and tried to speak. She put her finger to my lips as if to say "shhhh", and walked over to the door and locked it. I watched her walk back to me, her petite figure gliding as on air. When she got back, she stroked my head again and asked me, "Isaac, I'm here for you, do you miss me as much as I miss you?" I nodded ever so slowly as she began to disrobe in front of me, not believing what I was seeing. I tried to talk again as she bent over and kissed me, softly and passionately. I felt my chest expand as I took a deep breath and got aroused, while simultaneously reaching out and pulling her closer to me. She put her finger on my mouth again and slowly pulled the sheets off of me as she climbed on me. As we met, her head tilted back and she moaned loudly as she sat up, her beautifully bronzed body illuminated by star light. We then exploded with a passion I knew both of us hadn't experienced in years. She put her finger to my lips again as she swayed back and forth ever so slowly, her tanned body doing the dance of love under the cosmos. She then bent over and kissed me again and told me she loved me as her hair fell into my face. We then talked and hugged for what like seemed hours. As we held each other closely, we pledged our love to each other no matter what the future may bring.

"Isaac... Isaac... Can you hear me? Isaac!"

I heard a voice in the distance but couldn't make it out. As I lay there, the voice got louder little by little…. "Isaac, Isaac, can you hear me?"

I opened my eyes to see Diana standing at my bed looking down at me. It was then I knew I was dreaming as she held my hand. Dr. Brewer stood next to her, fully protected against the virus with his anti-bacterial suit on. I tried to take a deep breath.

"Isaac, can you hear me?" asked Dr. Brewer.

I nodded at him and looked at Diana. She was even more beautiful than I remembered.

Although I was sick, she looked perfectly normal. And it figured, I had a virus that was normal to her body chemistry. Since Virus' have been eradicated from our planet, her visit was safe.

"Isaac, Diana wanted to see you. Are you up to this?

I nodded in agreement as a tear ran down the side of my face. I tried to talk but couldn't. I could only clutch her hand, so I held it tightly as she wiped her eyes with her free hand. Her dark eyes were sad, and I wished I could help her, but I could hardly move. I was getting weaker and I knew it. I didn't want to die in front of her.

"Isaac, the Galactic Council has decided that Miss Aiello can stay with you while you are being monitored. She has agreed to do so, as she is under Isolation too and it would do no harm. She is safe as she can't catch what you have. But I feel obliged to tell you your prognosis is questionable. We are doing everything in our power to save you, but at the rate your red and white cells are being depleted, we can only give you three days at the most. Being a commander, I knew you wanted the truth."

I heard what he was saying and it echoed in my mind. "How could I die from kissing the one I love?" I thought. "What a cruel slash of fate!" Diana looked around the room and asked if her bed could be close to mine. Dr. Brewer shook his head in approval and two androids shuffled her bed next to mine.

The night was long. I stared at the stars while Diana talked and tried to cheer me up. While she talked, I quietly planned my funeral. When you are faced with mortality, your mind is open to a new room, a room no one has turned around in and returned from. You are made aware of so many things that one would never think about when healthy. You are actually standing at the doorway of death, an experience no one has ever returned from to talk about.

As the oxygen was forced into my lungs, I turned my head, and while looking at Diana, I absorbed the beautiful lady with whom I fell in love. Although aesthetically beautiful, her heart was so much more, a fine balance that esoterically few knew. It is said the eyes are the windows to the soul and the mouth is the window to your heart. She was graced with a fine balance of both. Her intelligence got her here, her beauty mesmerized me, but it was her heart that captured me. A tear rolled uncontrollably down my cheek as I thought of what could have been, but then again, I was happy with the short amount of time we spent together. Why and how we met is a mystery to me, but I would die a happy man with the knowledge of just knowing her.

Although on my death bed, Diana was a fountain of energy, a positive spark energized by a soul that didn't know the word "quit." As I fell asleep that night holding her hand, I didn't know if I would see the morning.

CHAPTER THIRTY-ONE
Chromosomes

The night was long. Having an open view to space leaves you with no time continuum. There is no sunrise, there is no sunset, just a changing cluster of stars as we travel through infinity. "I was born from dust and to dust I shall return," I thought as I saw the birth of stars and the ever-expanding universe. I would be no different. As I tried to sleep, androids came in every two hours to change the bags that dripped into my body. Thankfully, Diana slept soundly. She had been under a ton of stress for over eighteen months and this was probably her first good night of sleep since then. Watching her sleep was almost angelic. There was an aura about her that captured and harnessed energy at a level I had never seen before. She was a human dynamo with the voice of an angel.

At 0600, the room was faintly illuminated and Dr. Brewer entered the room and turned the walls on, turning the room into a soft glow. He walked over to the hologram and reviewed my night monitor. He shook his head and softly spoke into the recorder on his wrist. I couldn't hear him, but by the expression on his face I knew it wasn't good.

"Good morning, Isaac. I see you slept a little last night. But it looks like you were remming most of the night."

I nodded at him as he placed his hand on my chest and then my forehead. He looked at Diana and motioned her to go with him.

"Diana, can you come with me to my office? There is something very important we have to discuss."

Diana got up from the bed and walked around to my side and gave me a kiss on my forehead.

"I'll be right back, Isaac. Do you need anything before I leave?"

I watched her walk away with Dr. Brewer and wondered what was so important that they couldn't discuss it here? "What's come up? Am I dying sooner than he thought I would? Do they want her to prepare my funeral arrangements? What did he want?" I looked at her empty pillow and imagined her lying there, her sexy voice still echoing in my brain. I knew I was getting weaker as the time passed, but the fighter in me wouldn't let go. I didn't want to leave Diana now. In fact, I never wanted to leave her. How did this happen? Why did this happen?

Diana spoke of her faith often and tried to change my crass ways. I heard her but I didn't listen to her. I thought I was still indestructible. After all, I always did things my way. When I wanted something, I got it. Whether it was succeeding in the professions I tackled along the path we call life, or chasing a woman. If I wanted it, I got it. I knew there was a higher power, and I know I was saved from death a few times along the way, but the lion that roars in my soul has a chip on his shoulder and still thinks he's indestructible.

In the short time we've known each other, she has brought an inner peace to me. Though I have sought peace before, it has eluded me. As I walk this hallway we call life, the door to the room at the end of the hallway is getting closer, and may even be ajar. Mortality can change one's view of reality in a way that isn't perceived when one is healthy. Facing it makes me appreciate the little things more and makes me appreciate the gift of life too, for when the alternative is at your door, you realize it can be taken away in an instant.

It wasn't long before Diana returned to the room. She pulled up a chair next to me and began to tell me about her conversation with Dr. Brewer, "Isaac, something has come up. Dr. Brewer is familiar with Nuclear Biology, but is far more knowledgeable than I am, as your sciences have progressed. I understand his premise, but he has taken it a step further, a step beyond what I have learned. Isaac, you are aware that you have 28 chromosomes in your double helix, while we on Earth have 23. That is the variable here, and is the problem we have with fighting this virus. He believes that by extracting my DNA and mitochondria, we could possibly attack the human virus that is eating you alive by placing me in you. Because of your advanced techniques, there will be no threat to my life, but it is possible we can save your life."

I nodded and understood with a gleam in my eye, while I listened attentively. I felt hope for the first time in a while.

"Isaac, the transfer of cells has to be handled immediately. The virus has attacked your cell membranes, making it impossible for them to produce the amino acids necessary to produce the proteins needed to fight this virus. That is why you are slipping away. My mitochondria will have the necessary DNA to make their own ribosomes and protein to fight the virus. The need to do this hasn't been done before on your planet, but Dr. Brewer says the science will fit. I will be going to the operating room soon for its extraction. It will then be placed in a centrifugal separator for its injection into your bone marrow. It has to be done as soon as possible or you will leave me, my love."

Dr. Brewer then appeared on the wall. "I assume Diana has relayed my information to you, Isaac. If you're okay with this, can you nod?"

I nodded in approval as Diana squeezed my hand.

"Don't worry, darling, it'll be okay. Please don't leave me before I return. I want you to hang on. Do you hear me?"

I nodded again as another tear ran down my cheek. I couldn't speak if I wanted to, as I was getting weaker by the minute.

"It's time to go Isaac," she said, as she gave me a kiss and left the room.

Chapter Thirty-Two
The Operation

As I lay there, I was visited by Judge Lisko in a protective suit, accompanied by her android.

"Commander, I am so sorry to bother you in your condition. We have been kept current with your illness and the complications that have arisen. I have been selected by the Council to give our final report to you, hoping the news would lift your spirits."

I watched her as she spoke, but couldn't acknowledge her.

"We have already informed you that you won't be held responsible for your military actions or for your co-mingling with an Earthling, as your chip was indeed damaged and you were very honest with your replies. Your chip is being repaired as we speak. We have decided, as a group, that you alone could decide if you want the chip reinstalled. In doing so, a job as a Stellar Commander Professorship is yours, if you want it. But it would also mean your emotions would not be compromised again. We understand how you feel about Scientist Aiello and the option is yours. A choice Galactic University job without emotional feelings for Scientist Aiello, or a civilian job with all that it implies. We thank you for your service and wish you well," she said, as she patted my hand and walked out the door.

"Wow, she was all business! So cold," I thought as she left.

I laid there quietly as she spoke, not nodding or anything. I felt like I was going out. I felt weak. I closed my eyes and fell asleep. When I awoke, Diana was laying in the bed next to me, hooked up to an I.V. and sleeping.

"How beautiful," I thought as I looked at her sleeping.

As I gazed at her, Dr. Brewer and two androids came to my bed and lifted me to a gurney. They then whisked me down a hallway to an operating room where I was quickly anesthetized.

I was in surgery and the operation took less than an hour. I was then transported to the ICU, where I lay in incubation, and was to be quarantined for 30 days. During that time, Diana wasn't permitted to visit me regularly. When she did, it was only through a window. The doctors felt it was better if we were apart until the trial period was over, as I was weak. They had to know if the surgery was successful. Although we couldn't visit, just knowing she was there for me helped me a great deal, as the incubation period made me feel very lonely. Time passes slowly when you are infirmed. Your mind wonders, and you think of many things.

"How did we meet? Why did we meet? Two beings so different and yet so alike. The miles between us were vast, but with modern technology, it wasn't so far. Was it really the Browns' attempt at subverting our system for our meeting, or was it fate? Were we to be together, or was this the wicked hand of fate to tease us, or perhaps teach us? But what would it be teaching? How to accept love and loss? How to love and then go on in pain, always wondering if the relationship would have endured? Or was it deeper, did it come from above?" I thought.

The thirty days passed slowly, but my condition didn't improve. In fact, I was getting weaker and I knew it. The "wall" made it easy for the medical staff to observe my progress, or lack of it, but it also made it easier for me to see my condition wane.

I could use my memory device, and used it often. Diana occupied my mind, so most of my recordings were of her. All the while, I contemplated my decision regarding my chip and finally came to a conclusion. I would give up my mind-altering chip and the prestigious job at the Stellar Academy to live my remaining days with Diana, enjoying the love and emotions I couldn't illicit with the chip.

Then out of the blue, Diana visited me one day while I was in isolation with news for me. For the first time, she was also in a protective suit and we spoke through microphones. She said in order for her to live in our society, she would need an operation with her DNA manipulated to remove any other virus she may have that would be communicable to our population. Again, an operation that had never been performed before. This frightened me to no end. Altering her 23 chromosomes to fit into our 28 was an experiment at best. I remember the Browns did this on Earth with the Egyptians.

They actually created a man with the head of a lion.

Seeing the fear in my eyes and my vitals on the screen, and knowing I was a "cut to the chase" type of guy and didn't like drama, Dr. Brewer informed me that the operation on Diana was a 80/20 proposition, and the dilemma I was facing was just as dangerous. Frankly, they both were risky as they had never been performed before. I looked at him with a doubt in myself I had never experienced before. The man who had succeeded at everything he attempted was now in fear, in fear for his life and in fear for the love of his life. I then looked at Diana and tried to communicate with her, but I couldn't speak.

Dr. Brewer replied, "Commander, you knew the rules before you had a relationship with this Earthling. This is part of the collateral damage of that union. As we speak, we are awaiting the arrival of a specialist in the Double Helix configuration. We are doing everything we can to save you. Scientist Aiello will be operated on as soon as he arrives, and both of you will be sequestered until progress is achieved. I must tell you that your progress is in decline, and we are again doing the best we can to turn this illness around."

I stared at the cosmos above me when he got done speaking. I then realized my mortality and the inconsequentialness of my being. I looked at Diana and became melancholy, realizing for the first time our days may be numbered. Like the sands in an hourglass, I felt my life trickling away.

Chapter Thirty-Three
The Journey

For the next several days, as I lay there in my hospital bed, I wondered what would become of Diana and me. I felt no better from the transfusion, and the wall confirmed my suspicions. The operation did not work. I was dying, but I wondered how Diana was faring. Were the doctors successful with her surgery? Did she die? Will she live, or will she be left in a vegetative state? Where was she?

On several occasions, I watched as the team of nurses and doctors rushed into my room and began performing all sorts of medical procedures on the body lying in the bed. I could hear them, I could see them, but I couldn't communicate. Sometimes I viewed my body from the bed and sometimes I viewed it from above. I was coming and going. Was this a sign? An omen of what was to be? What could the Creator have in store for us?

And then it happened. Two days later, after repeated attempts to keep me alive, I, Commander Glock, had ceased breathing. I had succumbed to the virus, the virus I acquired from the love of my life. Will Diana survive me and have to live without me? After everything we'd been through, how could it end this way?

News of my death had gone out to all the mother ships and then across the galaxy. My funeral was one of the highest government funerals possible, and was attended by dignitaries from throughout our planet complex. I could see them, I could hear them, but they didn't see me. How could this be? I watched as my family and friends, as well as my superiors and subordinates, filed into the room where my body lie in state. My family and friends cried, while my military comrades stood ever so stoically awaiting the events to begin. After my death, my recording device was found and revealed my true state of mind and the love for my Earthling lover, Diana.

One of my recordings included,

"Diana, my pain is so great sometimes. I could see how I would like to close my eyes forever, but I'm afraid you won't be with me as I go, and so I fight on. When you are ready to close your eyes, my love, all the pain will disappear. Your senses will shut down and peace will enter your heart. If only we could be together again?"

My final wish, spoken with a weakness in my voice that was hard to decipher, was to be returned to dust and for the dust to be in Diana's possession.

Diana had been operated on prior to my death, and was in a room in the ICU across the hall from me. Because of her condition, she was not informed of my death. She too was struggling to stay alive, as her condition waned rapidly after her operation. It seems there was no way to adapt her 23 chromosome double helix to our 28 chromosome complex. Her body was actually beginning to get longer, and she was developing an elongated skull, an event that eventually resulted in her death. She was in great pain before she died, as her bones and skull were growing at a rapid rate, and she was bleeding from her nose and ears.

Her final wish was to be cremated with her ashes strewn across the Italian Alps. She left a clause, perhaps realizing her mortality, that if I did indeed die, we would finally be together. She too was a romantic, and held onto a note that I had written to her earlier at her bedside. It read,

Through the darkness there came a light,
A dim candle at first, then all so bright.
Soft spoken, not shy, yet pretty and smart,
You grabbed my attention, then captured my heart.
No one knows where fate will flow,
One thing is certain, you stole the show.

Immediately following my funeral, it was as if I was transported to another place. A beautiful place, a place I loved as a youth, a place where every day was new, where every day was fun. It was a tropical setting on an Island in Orion with green lush foliage and beautifully plumed birds flying so gracefully above. I sat there for what seemed hours just reflecting on my youth.

Then instantly, and soon after, I felt an inner peace as I was transported to another place, a place with a river as clear as crystal. It flowed majestically through the middle of the city, emanating from a mountain with a huge waterfall that looked like a bridal veil. The streets were pure gold and as transparent as glass. The walls of the city were comprised of every jewel imaginable and glistened without the help of a sun or moon. There was an omnipresent figure here, the Creator, and the river was lined with the trees of life, each yielding the twelve kinds of fruit every month.

As I sat on a cliff overlooking a beautiful waterfall that looked like a bridal veil, I noticed someone walking towards me along the golden street. The silver mist from the waterfall made it difficult to see clearly, but from a distance, it looked like someone I knew.

I watched her walk with a stroll I recognized, a confidence I've seen in few women. She then waved at me calling me over to her. Although I still couldn't make her out, I got terribly excited and my heart was starting to beat rapidly. "It couldn't be," I said. I stood up, looking down on her as she walked, and rushed down to her. She became clearer with each step I took. "Diana," I yelled, as we ran towards each other. "Isaac!" We met in open arms, with tears running down both of our faces. We hugged and kissed for what seemed like hours. But how could we tell? We were now in a world without time, without pain, without the stress of life. It was as comforting a feeling as anything you've ever known.

"My God, what happened? How long have you been here," I asked?

"It was strange, Isaac, I died a few seconds after you left. Somehow, I knew you were gone and that spark of life I had in me didn't want to continue without you. I then watched from above as they cremated my body and placed my ashes with yours. Then a strange thing happened to me. I could be wherever I wanted to be by just closing my eyes. The first place I yearned for was Monte Bianco in the Italian Alps, where I was raised. I sat on a hill and looked at and admired those snowcapped, majestic mountains and relived my youth beneath me. I could see France from that mountain peak too, and reflected on my youth and my family. I looked down on the beautiful river that wound through the flower-covered valley floor below and reminisced. My heart was at peace but grew somber because I realized I led that part of my life without you. Then I closed my eyes again and I was here. I don't know how or why, but I am here. Could it be that we each have our own heaven, or are we in heaven now? Oh, Isaac, I missed you so much!"

"My experience was similar Diana. I fought to live as long as I could. When I gave out, I too visited my family and then I was here. I can't say why or how it happened, but perhaps our Creator had something to do with it. Is this heaven? Do you see that waterfall, Diana? It looks like a Bridal Veil for a reason. Something in me is compelled to kiss you in the mist at the base of the falls. Are you ready for our next journey?"

About the Author

This is Patrick DiCicco's fourth book. He has written "Running With God," an autobiography, "The Jagged Side Of Midnight," a fictional account of a race horse, and "Youngstown, A Nostalgic View Into The Demise Of An Industrial Empire," a history book of the city. He has an A.A. Degree and attended Cal Poly, SLO, Cal State Northridge, and has taken Creative Writing classes at UCLA. He is retired and currently dwells in Solera, a Del Webb retirement Community in Bakersfield, California.

Made in the USA
San Bernardino, CA
06 August 2017